JACKDAW AND THE RANDOMS

JACKDAW AND THE RANDOMS

STUART DAVID

First published in Great Britain in 2015 by Hot Key Books
Northburgh House, 10 Northburgh Street, London EC1V 0AT

A CIP catalogue record for this book is available from the British Library.

ISBN: 978-1-4714-0469-6

1

This book is typeset in 10.5 Berling LT Std using Atomik ePublisher

Printed and bound by Clays Ltd, St Ives Plc

www.hotkeybooks.com

Hot Key Books is part of the Bonnier Publishing Group
www.bonnierpublishing.com

Also By Stuart David

For Adults:

In The All-Night Café: A Memoir of Belle and Sebastian's Formative Year

Nalda Said

The Peacock Manifesto

A Peacock's Tale

1

So there I am, sitting in Baldy Baine's Science class, staring out the window at a totally Z-list pigeon attacking an old sausage roll, when all of a sudden the Baldy One erupts.

'You, boy!' he shouts, and I turn round to see who he's freaking out at this time. Unfortunately, it's me. 'Look lively!' he says. 'How do you think I would proceed under these particular circumstances?'

I give the matter my full consideration.

'By sticking your beard in the Bunsen burner,' I almost say. Then I change my mind. The problem is, this is the third time he's asked me a question since the lesson started, and it's the third time I haven't been paying enough attention to know what he's talking about. I scan the room to see if anyone else is offering me a prompt, but they're all just sitting there looking thrilled it's me and not them in the firing line. Baine stares at me, the eyes blazing, and all I can really think of to say is,

'What was the question again, sir?'

And that seems to be enough for him, on this particular morning.

'Out!' he screams. 'Stand in the corridor for the rest of the lesson. And if the headmaster doesn't find you out there, I'll deal with you myself afterwards.'

Freakoid.

I take one last look at the pigeon, still doing battle with its sausage roll, and then I head for the door. Busted. There's a bit of cheering and a bit of laughing, and Baine goes off the head again, but by then I'm already out in the corridor and it's got nothing to do with me any more.

And then my life changes.

I'm just leaning up against the wall, staring across the corridor at this poster about not getting pregnant or something, when it suddenly hits me: The Big One. The brainwave I've been waiting for. An idea for an app that's so brilliant it's guaranteed to make me a millionaire. A billionaire.

I pull my phone out and go online to make sure the app doesn't already exist. While I'm flicking about I'm already thinking up names for the thing – the Minder, the iKnow, the Class Monitor? I'm firing on all cylinders, and all at once nothing else matters: not the embarrassment of getting thrown out of the class again; not the fact that it's only a couple of months till the first exams; not even the knowledge that I probably haven't taken in a single nanobyte of information all term long, in any subject. None of that can faze me now. This idea is going to set me up for years. For decades. For centuries.

It's total genius.

And then, just when I'm getting into the finer details of how it would work, my thoughts are rudely interrupted by the bell ringing for the end of the lesson . . .

Randoms start pouring out of the door beside me, most of them making some kind of deeply witty comment as they pass. Usually, 'You, boy!' or 'Look lively!' Hilarious stuff. I keep my eyes fixed on the pregnancy poster, riding it out, just waiting to see what Baine's got in store for me this time. But here's the thing about Baldy Baine. I mean, he's probably some kind of genius when it comes to chemical reactions and whatever, but that's about as far as it goes. His head is so stuffed with scientific know-how that there's hardly any room left in there for anything else, for all the normal day-to-day business like remembering to clean the food out of his beard, or for dealing with the pupil he's thrown out of his class for staring at a pigeon. So, basically, he forgets about me. I wait till the randoms are all gone, and a couple of minutes later my main wingman Sandy Hammil comes gliding out of the class and gives me the all-clear.

'Forgotten?' I ask him, and he nods.

'I kept him talking about protons for a while at the end,' he says. 'Then he just wandered away into the back room.'

I push myself off the wall and follow Sandy down the stairs, feeling pretty relieved.

'What were you up to in there anyway?' he asks me. 'You really need to start focusing. Two months. That's all we've got now.'

'I know,' I tell him. 'But it doesn't matter. I've cracked it, Sandy. I had The Big One.'

He stares at me blankly. 'What Big One?' he says.

'*The* Big One. The life-changer. The idea I've been waiting for. It hit me while I was standing out in the corridor. Baine's made me a millionaire.'

Sandy groans. 'Not this again,' he says. 'You're not pulling me into another one of your crazy schemes.'

I shake my head. 'This is the real thing,' I tell him. 'This one absolutely can't fail.'

'Like the bike thing couldn't fail? Like the disaster you pulled me into with the dining room trays? Like that couldn't fail?'

'Relax,' I tell him. 'This one's nothing like that. Anyway, I don't even need you on this one. You're off the hook. This one's an app. All I need to do is find a programmer who'll work for free.'

He looks at me in a disapproving way. 'Maybe if you paid attention in your computing class you'd be able to program it yourself,' he says.

'Maybe,' I agree. 'But if I'd gone in for paying attention in class I'd never have come up with the idea in the first place. That's what the app does. Stops you getting in trouble when you've drifted off.'

Then he says something that almost gives me a heart attack.

'There's already something that does that.'

I can't believe it. I couldn't find anything like that online. My legs go all weak and I have to grab hold of the banister and take a deep breath. Then I ask him what the thing is.

'Paying attention in class,' he laughs, and the good feeling starts to rise up in me again. I give Sandy a punch on the shoulder, and mess up his hair.

'This is it,' I tell him. 'This is what I've been waiting for all my life. This is The Big Time, Sandy.'

* * *

I'm Jack, by the way. Jack Dawson. Most people call me The Jackdaw. If they don't, I tell them they probably should. I look like a jackdaw. My eyes are grey, and my hair is very black, with white bits in it where the pigment died. Probably from the shock of realising what kind of life lay in wait for me when all this exam business started. Anyway, it looks kind of weird, my hair, but I like it. So I look after it. Get it cut feathered, and sweep it over. Keep it long and short. It's important to look good. That's my point of view anyway.

No reason to charge about looking like a Z-list pigeon, is there?

Not that I can see . . .

'What have you got next?' Sandy asks as we cross the playground, and I tell him double History, with Sergeant Monahan.

'No luck,' he says, and normally I would agree. Monahan is insane. But today is different because I sit next to Mark Walker in History, and Mark Walker is a geek extraordinaire. Whenever I'm stuck with anything in Computing class, which is most of the time if I'm being honest, I go to Mark. He never lets me down.

'See you lunchtime,' Sandy says. 'I'm off for an easy double in Hospitality.' And he heads for the stairs up into the old block, while I cross the playground in the other direction, flying high.

2

There must have been a moment, some morning or afternoon, when I actually chose to take History. What was I thinking? I certainly can't remember it now, and given the chance again I'd definitely choose something else. Especially if I knew I was getting Monahan. The rumour is he used to be in the army, before he started teaching. I don't know if it's true. I don't even know if the army would take him. I think he's too insane for them. He has very short white hair that looks like a toothbrush that's been used too much, and he's got a big round face that's bright red most of the time, usually from rage. His moustache sort of looks more like a cat's whiskers than anything a humanoid would have on their face, and a lot of the time he wears a bow tie that seems to be strangling him.

I wish it would.

Ten minutes into the lesson today, he already has Fritter Mackenzie standing in front of the class, off to one side, holding a big thick History book out at arm's length, for whistling while he was working on his project. I'm pretty sure it's against Fritter's Human Rights, but most of the things Sergeant Monahan does are probably against our Human Rights. Fritter's eyes look all kind of poppy and red while he stands up there, and every time he lowers his arms by a millimetre the Sergeant walks over to him and lifts them back up again until they're at a ninety-degree angle to his body.

'Start again,' Monahan tells him. 'Ten minutes without moving. You're only making it harder for yourself.'

Fritter's arms are all kind of trembly, and the book is all bobbing up and down. Nobody usually makes it to ten minutes, which means they have to stand up there for most of the lesson.

'I need to talk to you,' I say quietly to Mark Walker, as soon as I get the chance. Monahan has his back to us, writing something up on his flip chart for another lesson, but Mark still doesn't turn round to look at me. He just shakes his head stiffly and stares straight ahead.

'We'll end up out there,' he mutters, in a tiny quivery voice.

'Just whisper,' I tell him, but he gives me the head shake again and says nothing.

I look at him and sigh, then I tear a page out of my notebook and write, 'I need you to do some programming for me. In Objective C,' and pass it across to him. He turns to look at me as if he thinks I'm a total idiot, which he probably does, then he flips the piece of paper over and writes on the back of it.

'Do you even know what Objective C is?' it says. He drops it onto my desk and I stare at it for a while. Then I tear out another piece of paper.

'I know it's the programming language for apps,' I write. 'And I know I need you to help me with it.'

'But I don't know Objective C,' he replies.

'How come?' I write. 'You're in my Computing class.'

I drop it on him and he gives me the idiot look again, then shrugs as if to say, '*And?*'

'So we do Objective C in there,' I whisper, and he frowns at me then flips the page.

'No we don't, doofus,' he writes, and at that moment the Sergeant spins round, all on fire.

'Silence!' he shouts. 'Who's talking? Who has the gall to disrupt my class?'

All the blood drains from Mark's face. He goes as white as a ghost, and I look down at my desk, certain that his fear is going to give us away. I hit on the idea of staring at somebody else in the room, in the hope that Mark will follow my lead and mad Monahan will assume that's the culprit. I focus my efforts on Amanda Gray, but then I realise almost everyone in the class has gone chalk white, and it's obvious Mark's not giving anything away at all. I watch the Sergeant as he glares from face to face, then he notices Fritter is letting the book slip again and he walks over and takes it off him.

'Sit down,' he says, and he puts the book back on its shelf. 'This is now available if anyone else would like to come out here,' he says, and he glares at the zombie faces again. 'No one? All right. Let's keep it that way. Get back to your projects.' And he flips another page on his big chart book, and carries on with his scribbling.

Mark turns to look at me with narrowed eyes, and I quickly manufacture another note for him.

'I'm sure I've heard Bronson talking about Objective C,' it says, but I can't even get Mark to look at it. I have to resort to threatening to tickle him, which he knows will cause him to laugh his way to the book punishment, before he makes any response.

His lips go thin, and he starts writing. 'Of course he mentions it,' he scribbles. 'That doesn't mean he teaches it. What class have you been in all year?'

He leaves the note lying on his desk, doesn't even pass it across to me, and I have to lean over just to read it. I'm pretty surprised when I decipher the contents. Bronson bangs on so much about apps being made of Objective C I'd been sure he was trying to teach us it. I must pay even less attention in there than I thought I did. I know I zone out quite a bit, but this is pretty spectacular. I suppose that's the thing about being an ideas machine, you can't really see the sense in spending too much of your time listening to a teacher telling you about other people's ideas.

The main thing is always to make sure you're looking after your own brainwaves.

The double History feels like it goes on forever. A few more randoms have close shaves with the heavy book, but nobody actually ends up out there holding it. Emma Wilkinson gets closest when she accidentally drops her pencil and it rolls all the way across the floor to the other side of the classroom. She decides to go and find it without asking the Sergeant first, and he goes full scale mental. Emma makes such a hash of apologising though, even starting to cry at one point, that the Sergeant lets her off with a warning, and calm descends on us once more. When the bell rings, and the whole sorry ordeal finally draws to a close, I grab a hold of Mark before I gather up my stuff, and we walk along the corridor together.

'What about that retard gang of yours?' I ask him. 'Surely one of those guys must know Objective C.'

He shakes his head as if I've just wandered into his chess club and set up a game of draughts. It's a bit much, but I power through. I need to know whatever he can tell me.

'There's pretty much only one person in the whole school who knows Objective C,' he says. 'Some of the teachers might, but there's only one pupil.'

'I only need one,' I tell him. 'That's all I'm looking for.'

'Not this one,' he says. 'You'd be better off forgetting about it.'

'Who is it?' I ask him.

He shakes his head. 'You should dream up something else,' he says. 'You don't want to know.'

I stop walking and grab hold of his elbow. He gets a little bit of the ghost look again, although not quite as much as he had in Monahan's class. 'Just tell me who it is,' I say. 'Let me judge whether I want to know or not.'

He pulls his arm away and makes a show of brushing the sleeve of his jacket. I stand waiting, and eventually he says just one word to me, the name I've been asking him for.

'Greensleeves.'

I nod at him slowly and then let him walk away. Greensleeves. Elsie Green. Bloody hell.

3

The school canteen is over in the new block, so Sandy gets a head start on me lunch-wise. By the time I drag my terrifying sausage and onions over to his table, he's already halfway through his ordeal.

'All right?' he asks me, and I nod as I pull out a chair and sit down. He points his fork at my sad-looking sponge cake while he's doing battle with a mouthful of misery, and when he manages to clear some of it away he tells me I won't be needing the cake today.

'Why not?' I ask him, and he opens a plastic tub that's sitting on the table.

'Hospitality muffins,' he says.

They look good. In fact, they look so good I consider bypassing the sausage and onions altogether and just making a lunch of the muffins. I realise I'm pretty starving from all the brain work I've done that morning though, so I pinch my nose and get started on the main course.

'How was Monahan?' Sandy asks. 'Who got the book?'

'Fritter Mackenzie,' I say. 'Emma Wilkinson almost got it, but she started crying and Monahan caved.'

Sandy looks surprised. 'If I was in that guy's class I'd write to the European Parliament,' he says. 'He needs stopping.'

'Probably,' I agree, 'but the more time he spends on the craziness, the less time we spend on the history. That can't be all bad.'

Sandy takes one more mouthful of gruel, and pulls the tub of muffins across the table towards him. He opens the lid again and smells them lovingly, then he starts demolishing one.

'So what's wrong with you?' he asks. 'What's happened?'

'Me?' I say, suddenly confused. 'What do you mean?'

'The idea,' he explains. 'I know what you're like when you're on one. I shouldn't be getting a word in edgeways here, but you haven't even mentioned it yet. What's happened?'

'Ah,' I say, catching his drift. 'It hit a snag. I don't know if it'll happen.'

He doesn't look too bothered.

'It was pretty stupid anyway,' he says. 'Pie in the sky.'

'Grow up,' I tell him. 'There's nothing stupid about it. It's gold dust. '

He shakes his head.

'It's insane,' he says. 'It doesn't even make any sense. How can an app stop you getting into trouble for not listening?'

I consider laying it all out for him: explaining about the combination of voice to text conversion and predictive text searching. But he doesn't know much about any of that stuff anyway, so I just tell him it's all confidential, at the moment.

'Patent pending,' I say. 'But the idea's a peach, don't worry about that. It's the programming that's the problem. Turns out only one person in the whole school could do it.'

'How come you don't just pay a real programmer, then?' he asks me, and I laugh.

'Are you serious?' I say. 'Do you know how much that would cost? I'd have to rob a bank.'

I consider explaining the copyright issues to him as well, but it would be a waste of time. He's totally lost in muffin heaven for the time being. He holds his handiwork up to the light and turns it around, occasionally biting into it, and I start to feel envious. The sausages are all chewy and they won't go away. I let out a little groan and Sandy suddenly comes back into the real world and asks me why the one programmer in school isn't enough.

'How many do you need?' he says.

'Two,' I reply.

'What for?' he asks. 'Why can't you do it with one?'

'Because of who the one is,' I explain. 'I need two so's I can ditch the space cadet and just work with the normal.'

He stops abusing his muffin and looks a bit retarded for a minute. It takes him a while to unzip the data I've sent him, then he gets it.

'Who's the space cadet?' he asks, and I look around the canteen, over his shoulder at the geek table, where they're arguing about a pack of cards one of them is spreading out. Then I look at the table of popular girls, putting on lipstick and admiring their hair in tiny mirrors. I turn round in my seat to look behind me, and watch a sad group of teachers all staring down at their plates and saying nothing to each other, and I see a big gaggle of first years generally behaving like primary school morons, throwing bits of food at each other and shrieking a lot.

Then I see her. Sitting at a table on her own and staring into the distance with what I'm sure she imagines is 'poetic intensity'.

Elsie Green.

I turn back round to face Sandy and use my thumb to point at her over my shoulder.

'Her,' I say.

Sandy follows my directions, and I watch his eyes wobbling about until they finally lock on their target. Then his eyebrows go up.

'Greensleeves?' he asks.

'Greensleeves,' I reply.

He gives a low whistle. 'Game over,' he says.

'Could be,' I say, and suddenly unable to carry on with the sausage and onions, I push them aside and grab one of Sandy's muffins. They taste good. They taste really good.

I should have taken Hospitality instead of History.

4

That night, back at home, the Regular Madness kicks off for a while. It's been brewing up for a few days I suppose, but it still takes me by surprise. As usual, everything starts off calmly enough: I'm sitting at the table with my originators (Mum and Dad to give them their formal titles) and all three of us are just quietly eating dinner. Dad has stripped down to his vest, rolling pinches of tobacco up tightly in little pieces of paper, making a pyramid of fresh cigarettes for later on. Mum is still wearing her suit from the office, telling a story about someone else who works there, I think. I'm not really sure. I catch bits and pieces now and again, and it seems to be about a woman who lost a lot of money for the company by pressing the wrong button on a computer. Something like that. Anyway, that's all that's really going on. It's nice and peaceful. And then, suddenly, the heat turns on me. Mum asks me the million-dollar question:

'How were things at school today, Jack?'

I don't even look up, just nod. 'Fine,' I say.

'What was happening?' Mum asks.

'Well . . .' I tell her, inside my head, 'I had a real cosmic brain tingler: the one I thought would free me from having to sit here answering these questions for much longer. Then it turned out the only person who could help me with it is someone it's dangerous to go anywhere near. And who hates me anyway. So the whole thing went up in smoke, and now I'm back here answering these questions for the rest of my life.'

But all I say through my mouth is, 'Nothing much. Just the usual.' Which is obviously nowhere near enough for Mum.

'What subjects did you have today?' she asks, and right at that moment I can't even remember most of them.

'I had Maths last thing,' I say, and realise instantly that I should have thought about it for a little bit longer. If I'd said English, or History, Mum might well have left it at that. Just nodded and told me that was nice. But she's big on the maths. She sees herself as something of a maths expert, even though most of the stuff she got at school in the olden days isn't even the way we do it any more.

'What are you on at the moment?' she asks me. 'What were you doing this afternoon?'

I think it over, and I'm amazed to find it's a complete blank. I can barely even remember being there. I was mainly going back and forward between deciding I would have to teach myself Objective C, and then feeling convinced there must be someone else in the school besides Greensleeves who already knew it. But it blows my mind to realise I haven't downloaded a single piece of information.

'I . . .' I say, 'well, I had a lot on my mind today.'

That gets everything going nicely. Mum crosses her knife and fork on her plate, smooths down her skirt, and sits up a little bit straighter in her chair.

'Oh, Jack,' she says, then she appears genuinely lost for words. 'How long is it till the exams now?'

'Two months,' I mumble.

'But what could you possibly have on your mind,' she says, 'apart from that?'

'I don't know,' I say. 'I think I'm stressed.'

'About what?'

'About the exams.'

'Jack,' she says. 'Jack. If you were paying attention the exams wouldn't be a problem. You wouldn't need to be stressed. Can you see how crazy that is?'

I nod, and then my dad steps in.

'He'll be fine,' he says. 'Look at me – I didn't sit a single exam at school. It hasn't done me any harm. He can come and work with us. I'll talk to Frank Carberry about it in the morning. Don't get yourself tied up in knots, Jack.'

'Don't be idiotic,' Mum says. 'He's not going to work in there. He's made for something better than that.'

'Meaning what exactly?' Dad asks, his eyes already starting to go a bit wide at the outside.

'Meaning that's not good enough for him,' Mum replies, and although none of this is particularly pleasant I feel grateful that the heat has been taken off me, and that it's unlikely to come back again this evening. Normally, I would slip off at this point and just leave them to it. But owing to me losing heart halfway through the sausage and onions at school this afternoon, I'm absolutely starving. So I finish my dinner while they're jabbering away, then I make my excuses – which no one appears to notice – and I head for my room, where I lie on my bed and listen to the Regular Madness for about an hour and a half.

I went into the factory where my dad works one time. He forgot to take his lunch with him one morning, and Mum didn't have time to drop it off before she went to her own work, so she asked me to take it up to him on my way to school.

It was at the start of the summer, quite a warm day outside, but when I stepped inside the factory it was so hot I was scared to breathe. I thought I might burn my lungs. For the first few minutes I just held my breath, and it was so noisy in there I thought my ears might burst. It sounded as if a whole bunch of planes were all taking off at once, right overhead.

The woman who had asked me what I wanted in the front office led me down aisles and round spluttering machines. The place seemed as big as a city inside. It's a bottling hall: the place where they put whisky and vodka into bottles and then slap the labels on. My dad plays some vital role in the process of getting the labels onto the bottles, although I'm not sure what. When the woman found him he was standing beside this big long conveyor-belt type thing, tapping a bit of plastic up above it with the handle of a screwdriver. The woman prodded him on the shoulder and he turned round and saw me. It was too loud for him to speak, and I was still holding my breath, so I just held the lunch bag up to him and he gave me the thumbs up. Then I tried to find my way back out of there again, and got lost because the woman had gone off and left me on my own.

It was like being trapped in a nightmare or something. I kept bumping into people whose jobs seemed to be to test the whiskey, judging by the way they were staggering around and singing to themselves and everything. I passed a section where a bunch of people were just sitting sadly sticking labels onto strangely shaped bottles by hand. Over and over again. And I watched someone mopping up the broken glass and spilt whisky from a dropped bottle, and dumping it all into this metal bin, and then someone else came along and dipped a jam jar in there and started drinking the bin whisky, all full of dirt and everything.

I suppose you have to get through the days somehow in a place like that. I was just glad to get out of there alive, and school didn't seem nearly so bad as usual on that particular day.

It was quite an experience.

'It's a good living,' I hear my dad shouting downstairs, as the Madness continues to flourish. 'He could do a lot worse.'

'No he couldn't,' Mum shouts back. 'It might be a living, but it's no kind of a life.'

'What do you mean by that?' Dad asks her.

'What do you think I mean?' she replies.

'Do you want him to spend his life at a desk?' Dad says. 'All huddled up?'

'I want him to contribute something to society,' Mum tells him. 'Something other than liver damage.'

And on it goes.

The thing is though, I've been into the place where my mum works too. Quite a few times now. She's managed to get me in there using all kinds of excuses, but I'm pretty sure her real motivation is to try to get me hooked on the place, to let some of its charm rub off on me, in the hope I'll want to work somewhere like that myself one day. I have to be honest though, so far it hasn't worked. The best way I can describe it is to say it's pretty much like school for grown-ups. School without any of the good bits. In fact, it wasn't until I'd been in there that I even realised school had any good bits. But now I see that it does. Having a laugh when the teacher's back is turned, looking out the window at pigeons attacking old sausage rolls in the playground, just generally daydreaming and working on your crazy ideas. There doesn't appear to be any of that going on at Mum's work. It's pretty much just the sitting-at-your-desk-doing-your-project type stuff, slowly losing your mind from the boredom. You can't even dress like a normal person in there. No wonder the pigment in my hair started to die when I realised I'd be going to my dad's place if I duffed the exams, and a place like my mum's if I pulled off the miracle and somehow managed to pass them.

I'm amazed I didn't go grey overnight.

'People will always want to drink whiskey,' Dad shouts in the kitchen.

'They will as long as they're living with people like you,' Mum responds.

I consider going down there and asking them to stop fighting over whose world is the best one, telling them they've both been an inspiration to me. The only problem is, they might ask me what I mean by it, and I'd have to explain that I'm so terrified by both their worlds I've been forced to become a spectacular ideas man. I don't know if they'd like that answer. So I lie on and continue to listen to it, and eventually I come to quite a radical decision: I decide I'm going to have to bite the bullet and attempt to hook up with Elsie Green. I can't let her insanity stand in the way of my escape from this insanity. So I do what I can to filter out the Regular Madness, and call up my ideas machinery. Then I set to work on coming up with a plan that will somehow convince Elsie to forget all about what's transpired between us in the past, and do some programming to help me out on the big idea.

5

Success!

I even amaze myself sometimes.

One day, when I'm famous for all these incredible ideas I keep having, they'll probably have me on TV or something to ask me where my brainwaves come from. I'll have to tell them I don't know.

'What about techniques?' they'll say. 'Do you have any methods for bringing ideas on? A system of some kind?'

'I just try to keep the front bit of my brain occupied,' I'll say. 'As long as you do that, the back bit can get on with sorting things out, undisturbed. Then it just sends a sizzler through to the front part when it's ready.'

They might even ask me to demonstrate having an idea right there and then, in the studio, but I'll probably refuse. Not because I couldn't do it, just to maintain the mystique.

Does it mean you're going mad when you start imagining things like that?

Maybe it does, but the technique I imagine telling them about is exactly how it works for me, and that's exactly how it happened while I was lying on my bed waiting for the download on how to make amends with Elsie Green.

There was a spider up on the ceiling, almost directly above my head, and I was watching it trying to deal with two of its legs that wouldn't grip onto the paint up there. Six of its legs were doing fine, but these other two just wouldn't cooperate. The spider kept moving along a little bit, and forcing the two weirdo legs back up against the paint in a new spot, but they'd just slip down and hang off a little bit again. I was trying to come up with some kind of solution for what you could paint onto those feet, to make them properly sticky, when the solution for what I could give Elsie to get on her good side smacked me hard. It's just like I said: keep the front bit of the brain busy and the back bit will get on with delivering the juicy stuff.

It never fails.

So first thing in the morning, on my way to school, I take a detour at the bridge and head for the bookshop there, to start putting my plan into action.

It's open, but only just, I think. I'm the only customer, and the owner's sitting up at the back of the shop, eating a bowl of cereal and warming his feet in front of an electric heater that's blowing his wispy hair about all over the place. I stand amongst the shelves for a while until I begin to get dizzy, then I give up on being able to find anything myself and reluctantly approach the owner.

He looks at me as if I've wandered into the living room of his house, the little wisps of hair flapping up and down on his forehead as if they're waving to me.

'I'm looking for something to do with medieval times,' I tell him.

'Yes,' he says. Nothing else. He doesn't even say it like a question, just pops it out and then continues to stare at me.

I'm not exactly sure what to do next, so I just say it back to him.

'Yes.'

Then we look at each other for what seems like ages, until I'm the one who cracks.

'Have you got anything like that?' I ask him. 'To do with the Middle Ages?'

'Are you looking for something *from* the Middle Ages? Or something *about* the Middle Ages?'

I think it over.

'Either,' I say, and he starts up with the staring thing again. I'm just getting ready to give up on the whole enterprise when he turns away from me and starts typing things into an ancient-looking computer on his desk. The monitor is huge and yellow, with a big bit sticking out of the back like on my grandpa's television, but when I lean forward to see what he's doing I notice the screen is tiny. He glances up at me and gives me a look as if I've suddenly materialised in his bathroom while he's sitting on the toilet, so I lean back again and wait for him to give me the results.

'*Medieval Poetry: Love Songs of the Troubadours*?' he says, and I imagine handing that over to Greensleeves. Very likely to give her the wrong impression I think, and I stick my bottom lip out.

'What else?' I ask him, and he looks at me disdainfully and batters the yellow keyboard again. He stops for a moment and stares at the screen, frowning, then he mutters something to himself and punches the same key about fifteen times.

'*A History of Plague: Agony of the Black Death in Medieval Europe?*'

That seems to me a bit far in the other direction. It doesn't quite strike the note of reconciliation I'm looking for.

'What other ones are there?' I say, and he straightens up and moves away from the computer.

'That's it,' he tells me. 'Take your pick.'

'Two books?' I say, but he doesn't respond. He's already opened a magazine and started reading it. I screw up my face and try to think. There only really seems to be one way I can go.

'I'll take the poetry one,' I tell him, and he nods.

It takes him forever to find the thing. He goes over and stands in front of a shelf in the middle of the shop and doesn't move for about twenty minutes. Maybe his eyes move, I can't really tell from where I'm standing, but he certainly doesn't move his head. Then, just when I'm starting to wonder if he's got narcolepsy or something, he lets out a loud groan and stomps back to the computer. After some furious punching he calls it a 'butthole', and then storms over to a wooden cabinet thing where he pulls out lots of different drawers, hunting through all these little pieces of cardboard. Eventually he carries one piece of cardboard across to another part of the shop, and stretches up to a high shelf which he can't quite reach. By this time he's starting to lose his mind.

'What do you want this thing for anyway?' he asks me, and I tell him it's for a school project. He mutters something incomprehensible about school, and then drags a little set of steps across the wooden floor. I think it hits him on the shin or something because before he climbs up on it he shouts

'Arse-cakes!' in quite a high yelpy voice. Then he finally gets hold of the book, brings it to the desk to put it in a paper bag, and takes six pounds off me. I thank him and get out of there as quickly as I can, checking my watch to see how late I am for school.

Headcase.

The morning passes at about two kilobytes per second. Mega slow. I have French and then Geography, the two subjects I have even less interest in than all the others, if you can imagine that. There's one passable moment in Geography though when Miss Voss gives us instructions to read a few pages in our textbooks about snow clouds or something, and I manage to slip out my purchase to have a proper look at it.

Despite the kind of worrying title, I actually feel quite pleased with it. There's a drawing on one of the pages, about halfway through, of this medieval random standing underneath a window, playing a weirdly shaped guitar. And the thing is, he's dressed almost exactly like Elsie Green dresses. He's wearing these kind of puffy sleeves, and a waistcoat sort of thing, and some of the bits inside the book even sound like the sort of thing Greensleeves would say. So I decide I'm on to a winner.

Lunchtime eventually comes, and this time I've got a good head start on Sandy because Voss's classroom is in the new block. By the time he arrives I'm already three-quarters of the way through my soggy pie, and Elsie Green is sitting over in her usual spot, staring off into eternity. Everything looks good.

'I can't believe Murchison,' Sandy mutters, as he sits down.

'Nothing's good enough for that guy.'

He starts talking about something to do with a chemistry experiment, a test tube falling off its stand or something, but pretty soon he catches on to the fact that I'm not really listening.

'What's with you anyway?' he asks, and I pat the paper bag that's sitting on the table next to my tray.

'It's back on,' I say. 'I'm getting ready to do battle with Elsie Green.'

He turns round in his seat and has a look at her. She keeps adjusting and readjusting the strange hat she's wearing, and from over here it looks as if she might even be talking to herself.

'Good luck with that,' Sandy says, turning back round and pummelling his steak pie. 'Why does she dress like that? It's insane.'

I slip my book out of the bag and hunt for the picture I found earlier in Geography. Then I spin the book round and push it across to Sandy.

'No way!' he says. 'It's her.'

I nod and slap the book shut, then I pop it back in the bag and shove my chair out from the table. 'Wish me luck,' I say, and I get to my feet.

'You'll need it,' Sandy replies, and I walk off into the storm.

6

According to my grandpa, the best way to do something scary is to do it without hesitating. One quick move. He mainly applies his philosophy to removing plasters when you're a kid, but he says it doesn't matter whether it's a plaster or jumping out of a plane, it's all the same. One quick move. Maybe he's right. It's not how I decide to go about this thing with Elsie Green, though. Instead, I pull out the chair beside hers without disturbing her bizarre rapture, then I sit down quietly and clear my throat a little bit.

'Look at him!' she says, and at first I think she's talking about me, telling me I've got a nerve approaching her like this. But the madness that follows soon convinces me I'm wrong.

'Have you ever seen such unspoilt virtue?' she asks. 'And such modesty? He makes me want to live a better life. Look at how he blushes. Like the petal of a rose. He makes me want to do something heroic.'

I disguise my voice a little bit, in the hope she won't know it's me, and ask her who we're talking about. I have the idea that if we're already having a conversation before she realises who she's talking to, she might not just get up and walk off at the first opportunity.

'Drew Thornton,' she says. 'See how his hair cascades to his shoulders? And his eyes! Oh my god.' Then things take a turn for the worse, if you can get your head round that. She starts asking me if I can imagine the ecstasy of seeing such innocence disrobed. Something like that. Something that means can I imagine him in the buff, anyway.

'I'd give up twenty years of my life to bear witness to that,' she says. 'Wouldn't you?'

'Well . . .' I say, 'probably not, really.' And I'm finding the whole thing so bizarre I even forget to sound like someone else. Elsie turns round then and sees who she's dealing with.

'You!' she splutters.

'Hi,' I say, but she doesn't reply. She stacks all her cutlery and lunch debris onto her tray, and starts getting to her feet. I can tell I've only got a few seconds to save things, and I panic. A line I came across earlier, flipping through her book, suddenly appears in the front bit of my brain, and before I even really know what's happening I hear it coming out of my mouth.

'I come on an errand . . .' I tell her. Somehow, this seems to slow her down. She's still up on her feet, but her hands pause at the side of the tray and she doesn't walk away.

'Sent by whom?' she asks me.

I struggle. Another line pops into my head, but I'm not even sure where this one came from. I don't know whether it's from the book or not.

'By the king . . .' I say.

Not good.

'What the *hell* are you talking about?' she says. 'Are you mental?'

And there it is: I've been called mental by Elsie Green. Me. By her. It doesn't really bear thinking about. Maybe if I hadn't been in such a panic I would just have said Drew Thornton, and maybe I could have woven something out of that. I try one last desperate line of attack. Off with the sticking plaster.

'I've just come to apologise, Elsie,' I say. 'That's all. I really didn't mean to mess up your plans that time. And I've brought you a present.'

I take the book out of its bag and lay it down on the table beside her tray.

'Very nice,' she says, disinterestedly. 'Whatever you're after, forget it.'

'I'm not after anything,' I tell her. 'Just trying to make amends.' I reach out and flip the pages of the book. When it comes to the drawing that looks like her, I let it fall open there and move my hand about on it trying to attract her attention. It kind of works.

'What is this anyway?' she asks, and she sits down and picks it up. She turns back and forward through the thing, then she closes it and looks at the back.

'Actually,' she says, 'this *is* very nice. Whose is this?'

'Yours,' I say. 'If you want it.'

She looks at me suspiciously. 'You ruined five months of my life,' she says. 'That's not easy to forgive.'

I nod.

'I know,' I say. 'But it was a total accident. I had a scheme going with the bread rolls, and I had no idea you were going to be there chatting up Stoogey. It was just bad timing.'

She looks at me, appalled. 'I was *not* chatting *anyone* up,' she says. 'Especially not Stephen. How dare you suggest such a thing?'

I apologise.

'My mistake,' I say. 'That's what everybody said was going on. What was really happening?'

She straightens up and looks at the top of my head. 'I was attempting to woo him,' she says. 'I'd been working on it since the end of the Easter holidays. Then, in the space of ten minutes . . .' She stops, apparently unable to continue. She clenches her teeth and a strange little noise comes out.

'I feel your pain,' I tell her, with no real idea what I'm saying any more. I dig deep and come up with nothing. Then I give myself a sharp punch on the back of the head, in the hope it'll knock something into the front. It works.

'But maybe if none of that had happened you'd never have found out how you feel about Drew,' I say, and ever so slightly I think I see her teeth begin to unclench. She opens the book up again and has another look through it.

'This is really mine?' she asks.

'If you want it,' I say.

'*How many oceans* . . . ?' she reads, then she looks up in a strange trance, and finally fixes her gaze on poor unfortunate Drew. 'I'll take it,' she says, and I hand her the paper bag to wrap it up in.

That afternoon, sitting in Baldy Baine's Science class again, I feel kind of drained. It might just be the extra work my digestive system is having to do to cope with the soggy pie, but I get the feeling it's more to do with the time I spent in Greensleeves's company. It makes me wonder if I really could work on my idea with her, for the weeks or even months it might take. I might end up dead. I'm so tired in class I even find myself listening to some of what Baldy Baine is saying for a while. Not that I understand any of it, but his voice is kind of soothing. Like a boring radio droning away in the corner. It quietens down my head and stops me thinking. Gives my circuit boards a rest. Up until then, I'd been constantly going over the thing Greensleeves said to me before I got on her good side, the bit where she asked me what I was after. She was definitely on to me at that point, and I know things are going to be double hard when she finds out I really am after something. So listening to Baine chattering away about acceleration or something stops me driving myself a bit bampot, and gets me back on my feet again.

Halfway through the lesson I can really feel my buzz returning, and I start to feel good about how it went with Elsie and the book. I realise it's a case of mission accomplished. And then I have a fizzer. There must be something special going on in Baldy Baine's classroom, I think, some kind of hyper-charged atmosphere or something because of all the experiments he does in there. Whatever it is, that's definitely the place where I'm connecting with The Big Ones at the moment. And this One is huge. I'm just listening to him cracking wise about a feather falling in outer space when I see my way clear to how I can convince Elsie to make generous with her Objective C skills. After that, I can't pretend I listen to Baldy Baine much more. My leg's bouncing and I'm watching the clock, looking for it to perform some of those properties of acceleration Baine had been talking about earlier. It seems to be going in more for the opposite thing. The immovable force meeting the unsomethingable something.

But finally it gets there, and I'm up out of my seat before Baine has even reached the end of his 'Dismissed.' I streak out of there like Tom Murdoch did during our first ever fire drill, letting no woman or child stand in my way.

Elsie Green isn't difficult to find in the school corridors. All you have to do is follow the trail of giggling first years who've already passed her, and let them lead you all the way to the source. The fresher the laughter, the closer you're getting. I hunt around in the new block then the old one, till I find what I'm looking for, and I follow the laughter up the stairs to the second floor. It doesn't take me long to spot her. She's passing the language labs, and I turn and run back down the stairs again so I can come up the middle staircase and make it look as if I've bumped into her by accident. I'm kind of breathless by the time I get there, but I manage it and meet her just as she reaches the top of the stairs.

'Hi, Elsie,' I say, all kind of surprised, but she just sort of frowns.

'What do you want?' she asks me, not particularly warmly considering the present I've just given her.

'I'm just saying hello,' I say, and she looks at me suspiciously again. 'What have you got next?' I ask her.

'Double Latin,' she says.

By then I'm already walking beside her, not quite sure what classrooms are along in this direction, and not quite sure what to say if she asks me where I'm going. She doesn't though. She doesn't seem to care where I'm going.

I watch some of the younger kids staring at her as we walk, but she's oblivious to their attention. And to the laughter that starts as soon as she's passed.

'By the way,' I say, as if it's just suddenly occurred to me, 'you know what you were saying about Drew Thornton at lunchtime?'

She turns to look at me with narrowed eyes. It's pretty much the first time she's turned to look at me since I accosted her, so I take it as a good sign.

'How can you even dare to speak his name?' she asks me. 'You should be struck dumb.'

'Yes,' I say, taking a lesson from the bookshop bampot. It doesn't faze her the way it fazed me though. I'm not even sure she's noticed I spoke. 'Anyway,' I continue, 'were you serious about what you said?'

She does the narrowed eyes again. 'I'm always serious,' she says. She's right. Seriously mental. 'Especially when I'm talking about Drew.'

I nod.

'Good to know,' I say. 'So you meant it?'

'Meant what? That he makes me want to live a better life?'

'Not that,' I say. 'When you said you'd give anything to . . . To see him . . . I forget exactly how you put it.'

'Is this one of your schemes?' she asks me, and I shake my head. She screws her face up as if she's just sucked on a lemon. 'What exactly are you after?'

We've reached her classroom by then. She stops walking and turns to face me close to the open door. She looks inside the room and then back at me.

'I just thought I might be able to help you,' I say, 'now that we're friends.'

'Friends?'

'Well, now that we're on speaking terms.'

'I don't know what you're talking about,' she says. 'Help me to do what?'

'To see Drew,' I say. 'To see him . . . unrobed.' And I can tell I've finally got her interest. Her ears go kind of red, and a little muscle starts twitching at the side of her eye.

'Really?' she says.

'If you want.'

She covers her mouth with her hand. A couple of randoms squeeze past us to get into the classroom, then start laughing when they're in there.

'But what would you want in return?' she asks.

'Nothing,' I say. 'Well, nothing much. Definitely not twenty years of your life. Maybe you could, I don't know. Maybe you could do a little bit of programming for me or something. A bit of Objective C.'

She waves her hand as if to say that means nothing, and we stand and look at each other. My heart suddenly starts racing. It's going to happen. The idea is going to fly. In my delirium, I even notice that she's quite pretty, when you just look at her and don't see all the medieval finery.

'No tricks though,' she says. 'No photographs or videos or drawings or glimpses through a window. He has to be there. In the room. And so do I.'

I nod.

'Okay,' I say. 'And the programming . . .'

'After it happens,' Elsie says. 'If you make this happen, and it isn't a scam, I'll programme whatever you want.'

'Elsie!' her teacher shouts from inside the classroom. 'Would you do us the honour of joining the class? Please come inside and close the door.'

Greensleeves rolls her eyes, and I tell her it'll happen. No question. I turn to watch a bunch of first year girls giggling their way towards us, and when I turn back she's gone. She's disappeared into the class and the door's been closed.

'Is she your girlfriend?' a girl with a squeaky voice asks me, and I shake my head.

'She's weird,' another one says.

'I think she *is* your girlfriend,' the squeaky one tells me, and they all crease up, but I don't really care. I'm untouchable. I'm flexing my wings. Getting ready to fly.

7

For once, there's no threat of the Regular Madness at home that night. I go downstairs prepared for it, but it turns out Mum's working late, and it's just me and Dad for dinner. Unfortunately, that clears a space for an entirely new form of madness I haven't experienced before, and it starts with what we're having to eat.

'That all right for you?' Dad asks, as he puts my plate down in front of me. It turns out to be cold pizza and peas. Is that a thing? I'm not sure if the pizza had been warm and just got cold sitting on the plate, or if he didn't cook it enough in the first place. The peas are boiling hot. So hot I get a blister on my tongue with the first mouthful. He's spilt quite a lot of pea water onto the plate as well, so the pizza has the added attraction of being all soggy as well as cold.

'Pizza and peas,' he explains, as he sits down at his own spot.

'Is that a thing?' I ask him.

'It is now,' he says.

The radio is playing very loudly. That's the only way he can hear it, but he doesn't seem to have much interest in listening to it anyway. He seems much more intent on 'bonding' with me, now that it's just the two of us.

'I'll have a word with Frank Carberry about you in the morning,' he says, obviously quite a fan of cold pizza, judging by the way he's wolfing it down. 'Don't tell your mum though. There's bound to be something for you at the factory. Bound to be. Don't get yourself too worked up about those exams.'

'Okay,' I say.

'Still struggling with them?' he asks.

'I haven't had any yet,' I tell him. 'I'll probably be okay.'

'Not if you're anything like me,' he says. 'If you're anything like me it'll be a bloody disaster. Don't worry about it though. You'll do fine in with us. You'll love it.'

'I think it might be too hot for me,' I say.

'No,' he says. 'It won't. It's fine.'

'But what about in summer? I don't think I can take that. And the noise. How do you put up with the noise?'

'What noise?' he asks. 'There isn't any noise.'

'The noise from the machines,' I say, and he shakes his head.

'You won't notice that,' he assures me. 'You go deaf after the first week. That's another plus point. The sooner you get deaf the sooner you get your compensation payment – it's a nice bonus on top of your first year's wages.'

It might come in handy during conversations like this too, I think to myself. I have a shot at dealing with some of the pizza and peas. I don't get very far, but the attempt convinces me that it's definitely not a thing.

'So what do you think?' Dad says. 'Will I talk to Frank in the morning?'

'Leave it for a week or two,' I say.

'I'd better not,' he tells me. 'These things can take time. I'd better get it moving. It's not like you've got many other options, is it? You don't want to end up on the bins.'

'Well . . .' I say, 'I've got this thing that I've been working on. An idea.'

'An idea!' he says. He doesn't exactly laugh when he says it, but it sort of sounds as if he should. It's a bit like the bookshop bampot's 'Yes.' It's quite impressive. I file it away for future use. These things can really come in handy. 'Ideas are all well and good,' he tells me, 'but when it comes right down to it, they don't put food on the table.'

I think about saying there hasn't been any food on the table tonight anyway, but I don't bother.

He spends a while telling me a story about a friend he had in school. It goes on a bit, so I use my dinner to try to block it out, then I use his droning to try to block out the taste of the food. I go back and forward like that till I've managed to make quite a reasonable dent in it, and I decide that should be enough to get me through most of the night. I put my knife and fork in the finished position, and Dad's still talking.

'Blew his hands clean off,' he says. 'Blood everywhere. That's where ideas get you, as far as I'm concerned. Steer well clear.'

He picks up both our plates then and scoops the remains of mine into the bin. I notice with amazement that his is completely empty. As he drops the plates into the sink, he finally turns off the radio.

Hallelujah.

'I didn't realise that was still on,' he says. 'Could you hear it?'

'A bit,' I say, and he sits back down with a bottle of beer from the fridge and starts rolling up a collection of tiny cigarettes.

'What about tonight?' he asks me. 'Any plans?'

I shake my head. 'Just trying to work out how to get a boy from school naked,' I say. Or in your dreams I do, anyway.

In the actual real world I just say, 'Homework.'

And he nods.

'Don't work too hard,' he tells me. 'We've got you sorted now. Remember though, this is just between you and me – don't tell your mum.'

I get up from the table and thank him for the dinner, and he tells me it was his pleasure. Then I head upstairs to try to work out how to get a boy from school naked.

Here's the worst of it: I don't even know Drew Thornton. In fact, until Greensleeves pointed him out to me in her totally bonkers fashion, I wasn't even aware he existed. I don't know what year he's in or anything. The group of randoms he was sitting with at lunchtime looked as if they might have been in the year below mine, but I couldn't really tell. I didn't know any of them. So I lie on my bed for a while, amazed that I've managed to get myself into such an idiot situation, then I go online and look to see if he's got a profile. Hundreds of Drew Thorntons show up. I try narrowing them down by putting in the name of our school, but nothing shows up so I have a look at them all one by one. I'm not even sure if I can really remember what he looked like. Elsie said something about cheeks like rose petals. Cascading hair. What does that mean? I trawl through goon after goon, morons holding up beer bottles and hiking up hills. Pictures of cartoon characters and bum cheeks. What if he has one of those avatars?

Then I think I spot him. He looks kind of spindly, standing beside a monument or something. I click on him and feel myself getting a bit of a buzz while I wait for the page, then the buzz collapses. He's got his page so locked up I can't even see his friends list. Nothing at all, just his name and the photo of him looking spindly, and a message that he might have restricted access to some of his information. Too right he has. No mutual friends show up either, which makes me think this isn't going to be particularly easy, even in comparison to how hard I already thought it was going to be. I go back to my bed and lie down again, trying to think of a solution that doesn't involve sending him a friend request.

Then I send him a friend request.

I have a good look through my own profile before I send it, getting rid of anything that makes me look as if I might be a mad stalker. Or as if I might be asking to be his boyfriend. I change my picture for one I like in Sandy's album, where it's just me standing up against a wall. Sandy took it when we were on a school trip, and my hair is swept nicely. I think I'd just had it cut. And I'm smiling a bit, but not too much. In the one I had before, I probably looked a little bit insane. With this one he's sure to recognise me, and because I call myself The Jackdaw on there he's sure to know who it's from, if he knows anything about anything. I change my relationship status too. It was set to 'It's complicated', but that was just because

I wanted to write 'Married to my work' and it wouldn't let me. I change it to 'In a relationship', even though I'm not, just in case he gets the wrong idea. I leave my likes the way they are: 'Having ideas, and putting them into practice.' I leave my interests too: 'Making money, not being at school, and daydreaming.' My bio says: 'I am a serial entrepreneur with a series of disasters behind me, and a bright future ahead. I am destined to be a legendary ideas man. I like to dress well and I have good hair.' I remove the bit about the clothes and the hair, then I go through my photo albums removing the more dodgy ones from parties that could probably be misinterpreted. After that, I decide everything is probably in order, and I fire off the request.

I start regretting it almost straight away.

For the next hour I sit at my desk reading a business magazine, and trying to forget all about it. But I don't come anywhere close. Every three or four pages I go back to the computer, and look for the little red signal. I try to tell myself that nothing will come in tonight, that it could be days before anything happens, but it turns out I'm wrong. Within half an hour the red signal appears, and then I start to worry that he's some kind of mad stalker.Maybe he's never had a friend request before and I'm his first one. And now I'll never be able to get rid of him again. Whatever, I tell myself. At least I'm in, and that's all I really wanted. I can worry about the rest of it later. I hold my breath and click on his picture, and get ready to see what pointers I can find to help my campaign.

The first thing I notice is 132 friends. Reasonable. Just enough to make sure he's not some kind of loner who'll try to attach himself to me, but not enough to suggest he might be a major freakoid. I go through his profile, looking for more clues. Likes: 'Football, reading, Xbox.' Interests: 'Science, politics, astronomy.' *Politics?* For his bio he's written: 'I am in the school science club, and the school debating club. I live with my mum and dad and my dog Alfie. He makes me laugh.' He's listed a few weird books and films that I've never heard of, and in his albums it's just the usual rubbish from birthday parties and summer holidays. There doesn't appear to be anything I can use at all.

From his date of birth I work out that I was right about him being in the year below me, but I don't feel good about having become his friend just to find that out. And then it gets worse: I realise he's sent me a message. I think about turning the computer off and pretending none of it ever happened. Then I remember I've still got his friends to go through, so I do my best to forget the message and click on the bit to see all 132 members of his sad posse. The first thing I notice is that Elsie Green isn't in there. The second thing I notice is that I am now. A good proportion of the randoms in there are all called Thornton. I'd say about sixty-five per cent. Some of them are quite old, and some are very young. I scan through the rest and I'm relieved to find out there are three faces I know. Debbie Crawford, Chris Yates and Izzy Goodwin. None of them are friends in my profile, but I know them all a bit. None of them are weirdoes, which gives me a little sliver of hope that Drew might not be a weirdo too. While I'm still in that frame of mind, and before anything else can happen to change it, I quickly click on my inbox to see his message.

'Hi, Jackdaw,' it says, 'I've seen you around. Glad to be your friend. What's up?'

What's *up*? Really? I put the whole thing out of my mind and decide I don't need to answer just now. Maybe I don't need to answer at all. I turn my attention back to his three friends that I know, and start to give them all some serious consideration.

Debbie Crawford and Izzy Goodwin are both in my History class, with the Sergeant. Debbie even got the book once, and Izzy rides this kind of bright-green bike with strange ribbon things on the handlebars. None of that seems like it can help me, and there's nothing else I can remember about them that can help much either. But Chris Yates . . . He's in some serious trouble at school just now, with a lot more still to come.

I go on for a quick look at his profile, and I find it's wide open. The opposite of Drew's. I can see his wall and his info, and from his wall I can even get into his albums. He has no security at all. His bio says: 'I'm a bohemian and a freethinker. Life is for living.' Maybe that's why he hasn't set up any blocks on his page.

I spend a lot of time going through everything, particularly his albums. He's got a ton of them. All kinds of stuff. And each one has got a ton of different pictures in it. There are old boats and new cars and lots of foreign cities. Even his party pictures look more interesting than everybody else's. And then, in about the twentieth album, quite far into it, I find five pictures that change the game, that probably make becoming friends with Drew worth it after all. In my suddenly jazzed state I even write a reply to Drew. 'Just chillin',' I say. 'Glad to be your friend too. What's up with you?'

Then I instantly regret it.

I could have sent him a message saying the request was a mistake. I could have told him one of my cousins got into my profile and started sending friend requests out randomly. Now I've locked myself into it. I shut the computer down and tell myself to forget about it. Tell myself to focus. There are more important things to think about right now.

I sit with my eyes closed for a few minutes, just getting my priorities in order, then everything starts working again and I text Sandy to ask him if he knows where Chris Yates lives. He does. He gives me the address. I look it up on Google Maps and it's not too far. And without giving myself any time to change my mind, I shout to my dad that I'm going out to the shop, and then I head for Yatesy's place.

8

I was there when Yatesy's trouble first started. Then again, so were about three-quarters of the whole school. There were a lot of witnesses. I'd been down near the playing fields with Sandy, trying to work out the profit margin on this scheme I was thinking of setting up, when everybody round about us suddenly started running in the same direction, all at once. That could only mean one thing. A fight. Me and Sandy dropped everything and joined the stampede. By the time we got round to the playground in front of the old block the crowd was huge, a massive circle with a space in the middle, like an enormous doughnut. And standing in the space in the middle was this guy called Cyrus McCormack, and he was being hauled all about it by Bailey, the headmaster.

'Missed it!' Sandy said, as we threw ourselves into the scrum and tried to get down to the front.

'Who else was fighting?' I asked the girl next to me.

'Chris Yates,' she said.

And then, off to our right, about the same distance away from the centre as we were, Chris Yates suddenly jumped up in the air, propelling himself as high as he could go by pressing his hands on the shoulders of the random in front, and using them as a springboard.

'Who's fighting?' he shouted. 'What have I missed? Is it finished?'

It still creases me up in a major way to think about it. His face was bright red, and there was blood running out of his nose and a big scratch across his cheek. His hair was all sticking up on one side, and pressed flat down on the other where he'd tried to put it in shape. As he jumped up and down he kept trying to flatten the other side, but it wasn't really working.

'Who's fighting?' he shouted again, and then quite suddenly someone behind him grabbed a hold of his shirt and pulled him down.

'Wise up,' they told him, and they dragged him down low and wove him back and forward through the crowd until he'd gone.

Somehow, Bailey didn't notice him. Maybe everyone else at the front looked like Yatesy too. Maybe they were all scratched and bloody. It looked like it had been a wild one.

'Silence!' Bailey shouted, and quite miraculously the playground became almost quiet. 'Okay,' he said, 'I want the other boy involved in this fight to be standing outside my office when I get there. If he's not, the trouble he's already in will be multiplied by ten. At least.'

Then he dragged Cyrus McCormack out through the parting crowd, and hauled him across the playground towards his office in a way that was probably against Cyrus's Human Rights.

Needless to say, Yatesy wasn't waiting at Bailey's office when Bailey got there. Yatesy was in the toilets scrubbing his face, and trying to put his wild ginger hair back in order. ('Copper' he calls it on his profile.) One of his pals managed to get close enough to Cyrus on his way out through the crowd to whisper,

'Grass and you're dead.'

And Cyrus took the advice. He told Bailey he couldn't really see who was hitting him, and although Bailey probably knew it was a cover-up, he couldn't make Cyrus say anything more. Instead, at the next assembly, he uploaded an ultimatum to our whole year.

'If the boy who was involved in this incident does not come forward of his own volition, this year's school trip will be cancelled. I will give the boy in question three days to present himself. If he does not, then the rest of the school will be at liberty to inform me of the culprit in order to save the school trip. If I have to find out who the culprit was in this way the boy in question will be immediately expelled.'

Yatesy didn't come forward. In his defence, he had no choice. He was already on a final warning because of various past activities which meant he'd get expelled if he did. His friends have taken on a rotation schedule to make sure one of them is always standing near the door of Bailey's office, and word went round the school that if Bailey found out it was Yatesy who had been in the fight, anyone who had visited his office in the previous week would have Yatesy's crew to answer to. So far everyone appears to care more about the threat than they do about the school trip, and Yatesy is still going about his daily business. But everyone knows that the nearer the trip gets, the more certain it is that somebody will cave.

Now I've realised I can help him though. I've come up with

blinder. And as I stand on his doorstep, waiting for someone to answer the bell, I run through what I'll be requesting from him in return, and try to make it sound less insane.

Yatesy's room isn't like my room. I've never really thought much about my own room before, but after seeing Yatesy's I realise mine is really still just a kid's room. I still have a kid's bed, kid shelves, a kid desk. Up on the walls I've got one big poster of a jackdaw eating a coconut, and one of a map of all the different areas of the brain. But that's all I've really done in the way of decoration. My computer sits on my kid desk, and my TV sits on my kid chest of drawers. Piles of clean clothes Mum has brought into my room sit on chairs and things. A lot of junk lies about on the floor. Yatesy's room makes it look more as if he's doing a house share with his parents, rather than just living in *their* house. His bed is down low on the floor, with a sort of rug thing on top of it for a blanket, and it's a big wide bed. There's one area where he's set up his television on a stand, with two proper armchairs and a low table, as if it's a tiny living room. He's even got lamps in there. He's got a sink on one wall, and the rest of the room is arranged like an artist's studio, with all kinds of things that look as if they're set out properly. He doesn't have any posters on his walls. He has proper pictures in proper frames.

'This is a bit like my room,' I tell him as he shows me inside. He doesn't respond much. I think of saying it again but then I don't bother.

It wasn't all that easy to get in there in the first place. His mum answered the door at the beginning, and she looked like she'd have been happier if I wasn't there. She didn't really look much like a mum. She looked more like she was Yatesy's Art teacher or something. She asked what I wanted and I told her I'd come to see Yatesy.

She kind of sighed.

'What's your name?' she asked.

'Jackdaw,' I said.

'Jack who?' she asked me.

'Jack Dawson,' I told her.

She wandered off without saying where she was going or anything, but it was quite clear I wasn't supposed to come inside, so I stayed on the step. She was gone for quite a while and I didn't hear any talking, then she came back.

'What do you want to see him about?' she asked.

'Well . . . he's about to be expelled from school, for kicking this guy's head in, and I think I've come up with a peach of an idea for getting him off the hook.' But I only said that inside my head, while I was waiting for the arrival of the right thing to say.

'It's about the school trip,' I told her, and she disappeared again. That worked a charm. It was Yatesy himself who came to the door this time, not really smiling or anything, but I could tell I'd got his attention.

'What's the story?' he asked me, standing with the door kind of behind him and mostly shut, so I knew I still wasn't coming inside yet.

'I think I've solved your problem,' I said. 'I think I can help you.'

He stared at me quietly for a minute. 'What's in it for you?' he said. 'Are you after something?'

I nodded.

He thought for a while then stepped back in behind the door and opened it wider.

'Come upstairs,' he said. 'You'd better not be wasting my time, Dawson.'

'Call me The Jackdaw,' I said.

'Whatever,' he muttered, and up we went.

Yatesy has a kind of mini-kitchen bit in his room as well. There's a kettle and a tiny fridge up on the wall, and a few cups and bottles lying about.

'Want a Coke?' he asks me, and I nod. He opens up the mini-fridge and tells me to sit down. It's a bit weird. Nobody from school has ever told me to sit down before when I've been in their room. I look about and then go for one of the armchairs. He brings the Coke over in a glass and hands it to me. There are ice cubes in it. I'm not sure if there's something in particular I'm supposed to say.

'Cheers!' I tell him, and he nods, then he sits down in the other armchair.

I spin the ice cubes round in the glass and listen to the noise they make.

'Do you know Drew Thornton?' I ask him then.

He does the staring thing again for a while.

'He goes out with my sister now and again,' he says.

I take this as quite good news. It means Drew probably won't misunderstand my friend request and attempt to become my boyfriend. It also might help my plan a bit. I'm not quite sure how yet, at this early stage, but while I'm talking after that I keep it ticking over.

'Is he weird or anything?' I ask Yatesy.

'Weird?' he says. 'What are you, Jack? Like, six?'

I think of asking him to call me The Jackdaw again, but I decide to leave it for later. Besides, what he's said is probably good news too. It probably means Drew isn't too weird and I don't need to worry too much about having become his friend.

And I keep ticking the thing over about Drew going out with Yatesy's sister.

'So what's this all about?' Yatesy asks me, and I notice the kettle is starting to boil. He gets up and makes himself a cup of tea. Or maybe coffee. He doesn't ask me if I want one. I keep spinning the ice cubes round in my glass.

'I think I might be able to get a stand-in for you,' I tell him. 'I think I can maybe get someone else to say they were fighting Cyrus McCormack.'

He changes a bit then. He brings his cup of tea or coffee back over to the armchair, and I can tell he's looking at me in more of a friendly way.

'Are you serious?' he says, and I tell him I am. I think of quoting Elsie and telling him I'm always serious, especially when it comes to my schemes. But the idea starts to crease me up on the inside, and I have to struggle to get a grip on it again.

'I'm finished if I get kicked out of school,' he says. 'If that happens . . .'

He trails off and I tell him I know what he means.

'My parents would kill me if it happened to me,' I say.

He looks at me as if I'm retarded.

'Who cares what my parents think?' he says. 'They'd probably have a good laugh about it. It's art school I'm worried about. If I get kicked out I don't get in. I need my grades.'

I look over at the work part of his room for a while. There's a big easel there, with a blank canvas propped up on it. Hundreds of tubes of paint and a load of brushes sit on a table beside it. There are drawings lying all over the floor, and lots of other canvasses stacked up against the walls so you can only see their backs.

'I wish I was good at drawing,' I say.

'Drawing!' Yatesy replies, in exactly the same way my dad said, 'An idea!'

I need to start using that myself. It works good.

'I saw the paintings you did of Drew on your profile,' I say. 'They were good. They look like him.'

Yatesy snorts, and then he seems to remember what I've just offered to do for him. He wipes his nose and tries to pretend the noise was an accident.

'It's more about how the paintings *feel*,' he says. 'I'm not too worried if they look like him or not.'

I nod.

'They feel good,' I say. Then I decide it's time to ramp it up. I try to remember the phrase I found on the internet earlier, and I make my voice sound as mature as I can, in case he asks me if I'm six again.

'Have you ever used a life model?' I say. And what I'm really asking him is, 'Have you ever painted anybody in the nip?'

He doesn't seem fazed.

'Of course,' he says. 'All the time. Come and look at this.' He stands up and waves his hand for me to follow him. We walk over past the big easel, and he kneels down and hunts about amongst the stacked canvasses. Then he stands up and holds one out in front of himself. I can't see it from where I'm standing, and when he turns it round I wish I still couldn't see it. It looks like his mum. I'm pretty certain it *is* his mum. And she's totally naked. Before I can move my eyes I'm aware of lots of crinkles and bumps, and sagging bits. It takes me about fifty-three milliseconds to manage to attach my gaze to her feet, and nod slowly, but it's much too long. Part of my brain is already ruined forever.

'Isn't she beautiful?' Yatesy says, then he drops down onto the floor and starts digging through the canvasses excitedly again. This time it's much worse. He brings out a painting of what is probably his dad, and he holds it up in front of my face. 'Look at those lines,' he says, running a finger up and down the craggy old chest. Then he points between the legs, and traces a shape with his fingernail. 'Isn't that exquisite?' he asks. 'We could never invent the lines we find in nature.'

'Yes,' I say. I try to say it like the bookshop bampot, then I head for the safety of my armchair. Yatesy turns the painting so he can see it properly again and holds it at full stretch for a while, smiling contentedly to himself. Then, thankfully, he tucks it back where he found it and comes over to his armchair.

'Tell me what you want me to do,' he says. 'Let's get it over with. I've got an essay I need to finish for the morning.'

I lean forward in my seat, and do everything I can to block the horrendous image of Yatesy's dad out of my mind. This is it. This is my moment. I reach for the edge of the plaster. One quick move.

'Do you know Elsie Green?' I ask him.

'Greensleeves?' he says, but he doesn't laugh or have that expression on his face most people do when you mention Elsie.

'That's her,' I say, and he nods.

'She's quite eccentric,' he says. 'Quite intriguing.'

I let the dust settle, mainly inside my own head, then I tell him how I need her to do some programming for me. And about how she's obsessed with Drew. I tell him my project means as much to me as art school does to him, then I tell him the price Elsie is extracting in payment for her services.

'So you want me to paint a nude portrait of Drew for her?' Yatesy says, as if he's grasped everything without any problem.

'Not exactly,' I tell him. 'She says that's no good. She says it has to be the real thing.'

Yatesy chews his lip.

'So how can I help?' he says.

'I want you to paint Drew in the nude,' I say, 'and I want Elsie to be there while you're doing it, hidden away. With a good view of everything that's going on.'

I hold my breath. Yatesy picks his cup up off the table and looks down into it. Then he takes a long drink, looking at me while he swallows.

'You're a devious bastard,' he says when he's finished. He leans forward and puts the cup back on the table again, and asks me what happens if he doesn't agree.

'You don't get to art school,' I tell him, and I say it out loud.

He sighs.

'Drew's quite a shy guy,' he says. 'I don't know if he'd do it.'

I shrug, then the results of the thing I've been ticking over since we started talking suddenly sail into view. 'Tell him he should do it as a gift for your sister,' I say. 'Tell him it would bowl her over. Something like that.'

His face goes kind of red and I wonder if he's going to take it badly, but then it passes and he smiles a bit. 'Your mind is diseased,' he says. 'It's a sewer. But I think I'm starting to like you. You're creative.'

He sits thinking quietly for a few minutes, and I leave him to his thoughts. I drink what's left of my glass of Coke, even though it's gone all watery from the ice cubes.

'Tell Drew it'll be tasteful,' I say then. 'Tell him you'll do it kind of side-on, or something.'

Yatesy holds up a hand to stop me. 'Don't get involved in the artistic process,' he says. 'You're overstepping the mark now.'

I stand up. I decide it's probably time for me to go. I've done all I can here for the time being.

'Just a suggestion,' I say. 'Think the whole thing over. Let me know what you decide.'

I put my glass down on his sink, and start heading towards the door. He gets up and follows me.

'Who's the fall guy?' he asks. 'Who's going to stand in for me? Is it you?'

I shake my head. 'I'm close to a final warning myself,' I tell him. 'If I get kicked out I'll end up sticking labels on whiskey bottles for the rest of my life.'

'Brutal,' he says.

'I've got a few people in mind,' I tell him. 'Don't sweat it. Just don't tell Drew what's really going on, and leave everything else up to me. It'll all work out.'

He tells me that I'll have saved him from the handful of sleeping pills if it does, and then asks me what it is I call myself again.

'The Jackdaw,' I say.

'All right,' he says. 'The Jackdaw it is.'

He reaches out to shake my hand and I give his a quick slap, then I get out of there before he starts showing me any more traumatising paintings, of his grandpa or something.

Back at home, Mum is sitting at the table just getting started on her dinner. From the kitchen door I can see it looks a lot better than what I had, so I go in and try to steal a few chips off her plate. She holds up a hand to fight me off. She defends them well.

'Where have you been?' she asks me. 'Dad said you were only going to the shop.'

'That's what I told him,' I say. 'I was really round at Chris Yates's house, getting help with my studies.'

'Really?'

She's so impressed she lets her guard down and allows me to grab a few chips.

'Good for you,' she says. 'I'm glad you're starting to take things seriously. There's not long now.'

'Yes,' I say. Just like the bampot. And this time I get it right. She can't think of anything else to say.

I take a few more chips and she tells me that's enough.

'I thought Dad already made your dinner,' she says.

'He did,' I tell her. 'But it wasn't very good.'

'What did he give you?'

'Cold pizza and boiled-up peas. I've got a blister on my tongue.'

At that moment Dad wanders into the kitchen, looking quite pleased with himself.

'I thought I told you to make Jack a proper dinner,' Mum says.

'I did,' Dad replies.

'What did you make him?'

'Pizza and peas.'

'But that's not even a thing,' Mum tells him.

'It is now,' he chuckles, and goes over to the fridge to take out another beer.

'Be serious,' Mum says. 'You can't just feed him rubbish, Andy. He's growing. When I say make him a proper dinner I mean make him a proper dinner.'

'Here we go,' Dad says, and I slip out of the kitchen and head upstairs to my kid room, as the Regular Madness gets going all over again.

I lie on my bed and listen to it for a while, quite enjoying the normality. It seems preferable to living in a house where it wouldn't be unusual for me to paint both of them in the nude. I listen until they get on to the topic of my job prospects again, then I filter it out and start thinking about Operation Yatesy's Stand-In.

I lied when I told Yatesy I had a few possible randoms lined up to take the blame for him. I didn't want to give him any reason to believe it was going to be easy for me. I want to have him thinking that it's going to take everything I've got, just to make sure he thinks it's a fair trade. Over the next few days I might even make up some stories to tell him about how hard it's turning out to be. But the thing is, in reality, I know exactly who I'm going to ask. It's all under control.

9

All the time I had spent looking at Drew's and Yatesy's profiles earlier in the evening gave me a little mini-idea later on, once the Regular Madness had settled down and I was getting ready to put myself into hibernation mode. It occurred to me that if I could deal with Elsie Green online, especially when it came to working on the Objective C, I might be able to avoid her altogether in the real world and narrowly escape ending up in an insane asylum. So I got out of bed again and searched about for her crazy profile, then I zoomed off a friend request. Elsie wasn't anything like Drew though. I checked for the red sign a few times before I fell asleep, and I checked it once or twice before I went to school in the morning, I even kept an eye out using my phone in between lessons, but each time there was nothing. I didn't see her anywhere at school either, and the longer it all went on the more my mind began to play tricks on me. I started to imagine she'd found out about Drew being Yatesy's sister's boyfriend, and that she'd done something drastic. Swallowed one of those lover's draughts I'm always hearing about in English or something. It seemed like the typical thing to happen just when I had everything sweetly lined up and ready to go. The perfect way for my big idea to go up in smoke.

The more I thought about it, though, the more I realised I was probably just winding myself up. And I decided she probably just had a cold or something.

But guess who I did see! Or rather, guess who saw me. I was making my way from Geography to English, just getting ready to send a text to my potential stand-in for Yatesy, when somebody tapped me on the shoulder and nearly knocked the phone out of my hands. I turned round completely off guard, and Drew Thornton was standing there.

'Hi, Jackdaw,' he said, with a big friendly smile on his face.

'Oh,' I said. 'Hi, Drew.'

'Thanks for the friend request,' he told me. 'I just thought I'd come and say hello. What's up?'

That again.

'Not much,' I replied. Then something occurred to me. 'I was over at Chris Yates's last night,' I told him. 'He showed me some paintings he'd made of you. Looked good.'

Drew nodded. 'Chris is a genius,' he said.

'Anyway,' I went on, 'Chris told me you were quite a cool guy, so I sent the request. Just on the spur of the moment. You can delete me if you want.'

Drew shook his head. 'No problem,' he said. 'One of my friends said you were probably trying to scam me though. He says you always do that kind of thing.'

I gave him a little smile. 'Your friend might be right,' I said. 'I'm usually in at something or other. You should delete me to be on the safe side.'

He laughed. 'That's funny,' he said. 'What have you got now, Jackdaw?'

'English,' I told him. 'Hands Anderson.'

'I don't get him,' Drew said. 'I get Larkin. I'd better go. Arithmetic with Nelson. See you later.'

Then he ran off, doing a strange little skipping-type run. He's quite a small guy when you're standing beside him. And pretty weird and boring. It doesn't really compute that a little unnoticeable guy like that could lift Greensleeves to such a bonkers state of medieval passion, so much so that she might even throw back a lethal dose of the hemlock because he's going out with another little third year. I shook my head, and checked the time on my phone. I was running pretty late for English now, and late is something you don't want to be when you've got Hands Anderson. So I stuffed the phone into my pocket, forgetting about my text for the time being, and I made a sprint for it.

The stand-in I have in mind for Yatesy is my cousin Harry. I think he'll do it too. The only problem is he hasn't been talking to me for the past week or so. He hates me at the moment. I kept texting him all day, but he didn't reply. At break times and between lessons I scoured the corridors and playground for him, but I couldn't find him anywhere. I know if I can get hold of him I can talk him round. The whole falling-out was based on a misunderstanding anyway, and I know that once I have him face to face I can get him on board with the scheme. But he's a couple of years above me, and I don't know his movements. By the last lesson of the day (French) I was checking my phone almost constantly, looking for my acceptance from Elsie and a reply from Harry.

Eventually, Mrs Peterson caught me at it and confiscated the phone till the end of the period. I felt pretty jumpy without it. By the time I got it back I was having major palpitations, and I turned it back on and checked up on things as quickly as I could. Still nothing. From either of them. So instead of going home, I decided to go straight round to Harry's house, to see if I could sort things out.

He lives in the new builds, over the bridge and down past the roundabout. I always have the feeling I'm walking into a toy town or something when I go down there. The houses don't seem real to me. It's kind of strange.

I always forget which house is his at first as well – they all look exactly the same. But I finally find it and ring the bell, and it's the lunatic who comes to the door: my uncle Ray.

'Jackdaw!' he shouts as soon as he sees me. 'Get in, get in. I'm just burning some toast in the kitchen.'

He looks a bit like a bull, my uncle Ray. A bull with a big bushy moustache. I don't know if you get bulls with moustaches. Probably not. It's not a good look. He has two new additions to his appearance since I last saw him though. A massive black eye that's all badly swollen and oozy, and a big chunk missing out of the middle of his chin. He hurries me into the kitchen, where he really is burning some toast.The place smells like it's on fire, and smoke pours out of the toaster where two charcoal-black pieces of toast sit smouldering. Uncle Ray takes hold of them and throws them into the bin. Then he opens a cupboard door and clatters about amongst some glasses.

'Sit down,' he tells me. 'Are you drinking yet? Will you have a beer?'

'No thanks,' I say.

'You're still not drinking? Come on, Jack. What age are you now? Fifteen?'

I nod.

'I won't say a word to your dad,' he tells me. 'Scout's honour. Half a bottle?'

I shake my head. 'I don't like beer,' I tell him. 'It muddles my thinking. I need to keep my head clear in case a new idea pops up.'

He nods sagely. 'Understood,' he says. 'Forget I asked. What's the latest scheme then? Have you got anything on the go?'

'I've got a few things bubbling,' I tell him.

He sits down at the table, pouring beer from a bottle into his own glass. 'Let's have a little preview then,' he says. 'What's the inside lowdown?'

Inside lowdown?

'It's quite complicated,' I tell him. 'I'm working on an online thing, but I have to try and trick a few people into helping me with it.'

'You'll go all the way,' he tells me. 'You're like me – you've got the spunk. Have you noticed my eye, by the way?'

I try to pretend I haven't.

'Belter, isn't it?' he says. 'Hurts like a bastard.' He touches it lightly with his finger and winces. 'How about the chin?' he asks, pushing it out towards me as if I wouldn't be able to see it otherwise.

'What happened?' I ask him.

'Dissatisfied customer,' he says. 'Some turnip asked me to stop singing while I was driving. Me! "That's what I do," I told him. "You don't get in my taxi if you're not going to appreciate it. Everybody knows the deal." Not this guy. Told me it was giving him a headache. A headache! He told me to quit it or he'd make me quit it. So I stopped the cab, right there. I told him to get out, and he said he'd get out if I got out with him, if we could take it onto the street. So I got out.' He touches his eye and winces again. 'Mind you,' he says, 'you should see the state of him.'

'Is he bad?' I ask.

'Well . . .' he says, 'mainly psychological damage, I suppose. Badly scarred emotionally.' He laughs. 'Anyway, all's well that ends well. We both got back into the cab when the thing was over, and he gave me a nice enough tip when I dropped him off. Even joined in with the singing for a wee while. Told me I wasn't really all that bad. Cheeky bastard. Not all that bad! I could've been the next Pavarotti.'

He's always saying that. I don't know if it's true. I don't really know who Pavarotti is. Maybe he could have been, if Pavarotti is someone who can't really sing.

'So what brings you to this corner of paradise?' he asks me. 'Come to see your cousin?'

I nod. 'I couldn't find him in school,' I say.

Uncle Ray drains most of the beer out of his glass, slurping and burping. Then he wipes his moustache. 'He should be back soon,' he says. 'Mind you, I say that, but Christ knows where he is. We're not talking at the minute. I've had it with him, to be honest. I should speak to your dad, see if he'll do a swap. How come I wind up with the idiot? You should come and live here, Jack. We'd have a laugh together.'

He reaches across the table and rubs my hair, more or less ruining the perfect sweep I had going on. He sort of embarrasses and terrifies me at the same time, my uncle Ray.

'Me and The Jackdaw!' he says. 'What a team!'

A few minutes later the front door opens, and Uncle Ray puts a finger up to his lips. I hear Harry clumping along the hallway and then dumping his bag at the bottom of the stairs. He takes his coat off and I hear that going up on the rack, then he carries on into the kitchen. You can tell he isn't expecting anyone to be there, and he jumps a bit when he sees us. He looks kind of startled, then when he realises I'm there he turns round and walks back out again. We hear him stomping up the stairs and then going into his room.

'Must be Tampon Time,' Uncle Ray says. 'He didn't look too happy to see *you* either.'

'We fell out a couple of weeks ago,' I tell him. 'Just a misunderstanding. I've come to sort it out.'

'Good luck with that,' Uncle Ray says, and he takes his glass across to the sink and rinses it out. Then he puts another couple of pieces of bread into the still smoking toaster. I get up from the table and push my chair in.

'See you later, Uncle Ray,' I say, and then I make my way up to Harry's room, and knock lightly on his door.

10

My cousin Harry's room is just like mine, a kid room. He still has a poster of a dragon above his bed, and over on the other wall he has a chart for this game he plays on the computer. He even still has a few toys lying about that he's never bothered to throw out. Sad. His room really makes me want to fix up mine.

While I stand at the door looking around at all this stuff, Harry sits at his desk glaring at me. He didn't answer my knock on the door, so I just came in, but it's clear he's not too happy about it.

'Beat it!' he tells me. 'I haven't got anything to say to you.'

'Maybe I've got something to say to you though,' I reply. 'Maybe I've come to apologise.'

'Did you bring my iPad?' he asks me, and I shake my head. 'Beat it, then. I'm not interested.'

I close the door and come a bit further into the room. Harry turns away from me and hunches over the books that are lying open on his desk, pretending he's getting to work on something. I go over and sit down on his kid bed.

'I've brought you something to make up for the iPad,' I say. 'I'm still trying to get that back, but I've brought you something better in the meantime.'

That gets his attention. He abandons the books and spins his swivel chair, then he looks over at me.

'Let's see it,' he says, and he wheels the chair halfway over towards me.

I get up off the bed. 'It's not something you can see,' I tell him, turning my back to him and studying some of the sad debris he's got on his shelves. 'It's an opportunity.'

I hear the chair rolling back towards the desk again. 'Forget it,' he says. 'I'm not interested in your schemes, Dawson.'

'Call me The Jackdaw,' I say.

'How about I call you The Jackass?' he replies.

'Okay,' I say. 'Dawson's fine. Whatever.'

'How about I call you a cab?' Harry continues. 'I want you out of here, Jackass. I'll give you thirty seconds, then I'm shouting on mad Ray to give you a lift home. Opera all the way.'

'That's quite a black eye he's wearing,' I say, but Harry doesn't reply. So I tell him I'm sorry about the iPad. For about the five hundredth time. 'It was a misunderstanding,' I tell him. 'That's all.'

He turns round with his face red. 'I gave you a loan of my iPad and you sold it. Where's the misunderstanding?'

'I didn't sell it,' I say. 'How many times do I have to tell you that? I lost it in a bet. And the misunderstanding is I thought you'd given me it to keep.'

'No you didn't,' Harry shouts. 'You asked me if you could borrow it, and I told you not to break it. How can that possibly imply I was giving you it to keep?'

'That's not what happened,' I tell him. 'You know it's not.'

He sighs very loudly and then slams his books about on the desk, making out as if this is him finally settling down to work. I walk towards the door and open it a bit.

'I'll see you later,' I say. 'I had the perfect plan to get you to university, but if you'd rather have the iPad it's your loss.'

I open the door a little more but I can already hear him stirring behind me. The chair creaks as it turns, even though he's trying his best to keep it quiet. I open the door a bit further and step out into the hall, then I start closing the door behind me.

'Hang on,' Harry says quietly. 'Come back a minute. Maybe I am interested.'

'Make your mind up,' I say.

'Let's hear it,' he says. 'I'm listening. The iPad can wait. Come back in and tell me the scheme.'

I hover with the doorknob in my hand for a while, just to keep him in suspense, then I pretend I'm quite exasperated by the whole business, and I come back into the room.

Harry doesn't know anything about the trouble Yatesy is in. He remembers the fight, particularly the part where Yatesy jumped up and down asking what was happening, but he doesn't know anything about the threat to the school trip or about Bailey's ultimatum. His year isn't affected by it, and Harry isn't the most in-touch person anyway, so I have to fill him in a bit.

'What's any of this got to do with me, though?' he says, quite early on. 'This is starting to look like a scam to make me forget about the iPad.'

'Relax,' I say. 'I'm giving you a gift. I thought all that mattered to you was getting to university?'

He shakes his head. 'That's finished,' he says. 'Ray says I can forget it. He says I'm already enough of an embarrassment as it is, and there's no way he's letting me study catering. He says he wants to see proof I'm a man. He's trying to force me to finish with school right now, and start working on the taxis.'

'That's why this is perfect for you,' I say. 'This is exactly what you're looking for. Yatesy's about to be expelled. If he doesn't step up and admit he was in that fight, somebody else will spill the beans to save the school trip. The only thing that can keep both sides happy is a stand-in. Now, if you were to come forward . . .'

'I'd get expelled.'

I shake my head. 'Yatesy's on a final warning,' I say. 'That's the only reason he'd get expelled. How many warnings have you ever had? Apart from being warned you might burst your brains from studying too much? You'd only get suspended.'

At first he doesn't respond. He gets up out of his chair and paces round the room a bit.

'Just imagine how proud your dad will be,' I say. 'Not only have you been in a proper fight for the first time in your life, you've been suspended from school for it as well. Imagine him being able to tell his taxi pals about that. Imagine him being able to hammer on about it down at the bowling club. Suddenly you're a man. He'll be all over you. And then you can talk him into letting you do whatever you want at university.'

He keeps pacing.

'Besides—' I say, and he tells me to shut up.

'Let me think for a minute,' he says. 'Stop talking.' So I stop talking and let him think. I pick up this sort of dinosaur thing he's got on his chest of drawers and start playing with it.

'I hate your schemes,' he says suddenly. 'They're moronic. They always make me feel sick. But this one . . .'

I keep playing with the dinosaur and ignore the insult. I can tell something's starting to happen.

'What if somebody comes forward and tells Bailey I wasn't in the fight? What then?'

'Who would do that?' I say. 'Who would risk getting their head kicked in when the school trip's already been saved? It doesn't make any sense.'

I put the dinosaur down and turn to look at him. There's a slight smile making his mouth twitch at the corners.

'Okay,' he says. 'Okay, I'll do it.'

'You will?'

He nods. 'I will. On one condition.'

I feel a bit stunned.

'What are you talking about?' I ask.

'I'll do it as soon as you get my iPad back,' he says. 'The minute I've got that in my hand, I'll march into Bailey's office and tell him it was me who fought Cyrus McCormack.'

'No,' I say. 'No. That's not what's happening here, Harry. I'm giving you this to make up for the iPad. You're the one who benefits from this.'

'So you say.'

'What the hell are you talking about?'

'I'm on to you,' he says. 'I know there's something in this for you. I can feel it. I'm your cousin – I know how your mind works.'

'*What?*' I say. 'That's not even a thing. Since when did *cousins* know how each other's minds work?'

'Since now,' he says. 'Since whenever. I know how *your* mind works, that's all that matters. I know there's something in this for you. What do you care about Yatesy? You don't even go on school trips. You've got it set up so Yatesy has to give you something if you find a stand-in for him.'

'No I haven't.'

'Okay then,' Harry says. 'Fair enough. But I don't think I'll do it. It might not work anyway. Ray probably still won't let me go to university, and I might end up getting expelled.'

'No you won't,' I say. 'I promise. You've got to try it, Harry.'

He grins at me. It's not a pretty picture. 'Why do you care?' he asks. 'What does it matter to you if I end up being a chef or a taxi driver? Don't act it.'

He's got me. I hunt around in the back bit of my brain for something to help me out, but it's completely empty. I give myself a little bump back there and try to knock an idea forward, but nothing happens.

'So what's he going to give you?' Harry asks.

I sigh. 'He's going to get somebody to help me with some programming, for this idea I've got.'

'Bingo,' Harry says. 'I knew it. I knew you weren't doing this to help me.'

'I came to you first though,' I tell him. 'There are plenty of other randoms I could've gone to. I'm offering it to you to help you out of a jam.'

'I appreciate that,' Harry says. 'And I'm willing to do it. It might even work. But I'm only doing it if you agree to my condition. Take it or leave it.'

I know I'm going to have to take it, but I try one more line of attack. 'It's a time-sensitive operation though,' I explain. 'Somebody could come forward and tell Bailey it was Yatesy who was fighting at any minute. Then we've both had it. You're back to square one with your dad, and I've got nobody to help me with my idea.'

'Exactly,' Harry says. 'So you'd better get a move on.'

'But surely it's safer if you go to Bailey straight away, and I get the iPad back as soon as I can?'

Harry shakes his head. 'This is Friday,' he says. 'Who's going to go to Bailey over the weekend? That gives you two days to get the iPad back, then I can go to Bailey first thing on Monday morning.'

'What if someone gets there before you?'

'I'll turn up at school before it opens. I'll be waiting outside Bailey's door when he arrives. It's your choice, Jack.'

I hold his gaze. I think of what it all means. If I get him his iPad, he'll get Yatesy off the hook. Once Yatesy's off the hook, he'll get Drew Thornton in the buff for me. Once Elsie Green's seen Drew in the buff, she'll program the Objective C for me, and once she's programmed the Objective C I'll be a millionaire. Maybe even a billionaire. It seems like a small price to pay, so I finally agree to his terms.

'It has to be *my* iPad though,' he says. 'There's stuff on there I need. Don't go thinking you can just steal somebody else's, or buy me one from somewhere.'

'All right,' I say. 'It's a deal. I'll be round with it on Sunday night. At the latest.' He looks at me as if he believes me, and I find it quite hard to keep eyeballing him. The truth is, I'm not entirely sure I believe it myself.

* * *

Uncle Ray offers to drive me home, but I tell him I'm just going a few doors down to see another friend. I can't face the singing, not after the brain drain I've been through with Harry. I need some time on my own to clear my head, and to let the ideas start forming about how I'm going to get that iPad back.

'Tell your dad I said hello,' Uncle Ray says, and he punches me, quite hard, on the top of the arm. 'Tell him he's a lucky bastard to have a boy like you.'

'I will,' I say, then I start walking home. I check my phone to see if Elsie Green has accepted my friend request yet, but the red circle is still nowhere to be seen.

11

So there I am, lying on the couch with a major brain freeze on, when my dad sneaks into the room like an animal trapper and taps me on the shoulder. It's Sunday afternoon, and I've been working on a solution to the iPad fiasco all weekend, but I've drawn a complete blank. I've been using all my best methods to occupy the front bit of my brain, mind-mapping, free-writing, rearranging the furniture in my room. I've even tried falling asleep, in the hope that I would wake up with a solution. Nothing.

'Where's your mum?' Dad whispers, as I lie there staring up at him.

'At the shops,' I say.

'Good,' he whispers, and he signals me to follow him by moving his index finger, as if we're both in a midnight jungle, hunting down tigers using night vision.

'What is it?' I ask him.

He just does the finger thing again, and goes over to the dining table at the top of the room, the one we never use unless my grandpa is visiting.

I struggle into a sitting position, and wait for the brain fog to pass, then I follow him. By the time I sit down, he's taken out this strange mechanical contraption and he's feeding one of his cigarette papers into it, dropping tobacco into the top. He turns a handle and the paper sort of shoots out, all crumpled up. Then the tobacco falls onto the table.

'Crap,' he says, very quietly, and he reaches for a new cigarette paper.

'What are you whispering for?' I ask him, and he pokes around in his tin for another bit of tobacco.

'Am I whispering?' he asks.

I nod.

'Sorry,' he says, but he continues to whisper anyway. 'I just don't want your mum to hear this.'

'She's at the shops,' I tell him. 'How can she hear you from the shops?'

'I'm not taking any chances,' he says, and has another go at turning his little handle. This time a cigarette drops onto the table. It looks kind of fat, and the tobacco doesn't nearly fill it, but it's still recognisable as a cigarette.

'Ta-da!' Dad whispers. 'How about that?'

He puts it in his mouth and lights it, and a huge flame shoots up towards the bit of hair that covers his brow.

'Jesus Christ!' he shouts, loud enough for Mum to hear wherever she is. He drops the cigarette on the table and starts slapping at his head, then he picks up his tobacco tin and starts hitting the cigarette with it. Eventually the cigarette goes out, and his hair stops smouldering. He picks up the tin and tries to see his reflection in it, then he puffs up his cheeks and sets about rolling one of his tight little cigarettes in the normal way, and lights it up. His burnt hair smells kind of weird.

'Is that what you wanted to show me?' I ask him, when things have calmed down.

He puts the contraption away in his pocket and shakes his head. 'That's just something I'm trying out,' he says, whispering again now. 'Takes a bit of getting used to.'

He taps some ash off the end of the handmade cigarette, then holds it up and looks at it in a satisfied way.

'All right,' he says, 'Now. Back to business. By the way, don't mention any of this to your mum.' He looks about the room, as if I might have been lying to him, and she's really hiding behind the door or underneath one of the armchairs.

'The fire?' I ask.

'Not the fire,' he says. 'The thing I'm about to tell you. Anyway, it wasn't a fire. Just a minor mishap. Teething problems.' He rubs his hair and puts the pieces of the disaster cigarette in the ashtray, then picks at the mark its flame has left on the table. 'Come to think of it,' he says, 'don't tell her about the fire either. She'll kill me if she sees that burn mark.'

'Okay,' I say, 'I won't. I'd better go upstairs now and get on with some things though.'

It's a good effort, quite inspired I think, but it doesn't work. Dad shakes his head.

'Stay here,' he says, then he gets up, goes out into the hall and comes back holding a piece of paper. He drops it in front of me and sits down again.

'I had a word with Frank Carberry,' he says. He's speaking so quietly now I have to lean a bit closer just to hear him. 'There's something on the go right now. In the warehouse. He said to send you in and they'll give you a good hearing.'

The room starts to spin uncontrollably.

Dad stretches across the table and puts his finger on the piece of paper. I haven't dared to look at it yet; at first I thought it might be something bad from school. Now I wish it was.

'Everything's on here,' Dad tells me, and he runs his finger along the words as he reads them out, upside down for him, the right way up for me. It's as if he thinks the stories about how little attention I pay in class have been undersold. He seems to think I can't even read.

'Nine thirty a.m., Tuesday morning,' he whispers. 'The admin office. Mrs Mary McGowan.' That's all it says on the paper. He stops reading and sits back in his chair again, while I stare down at the page. 'Mary McGowan,' Dad says. 'That's who'll be interviewing you. She knows you're my boy, so just be yourself and everything'll be fine. And don't tell your mum about it – you know what she's like. She'll put the kybosh on it before you even set foot in there.'

'I should bloody hope so!' I shout. Inwardly. Outwards I just say, 'But I'll have to tell her.'

'No you won't,' Dad says.

My brain flaps around as if it's a fish stuck on the beach, trying to get back into the water.

'I've got school on Tuesday morning,' I say. 'She'll find out if I don't go.'

'I'll write you a note,' Dad says. 'Don't worry too much about your mum.' He glances towards the door again, and has a quick check underneath the armchairs. 'You're old enough to make your own decisions now.'

'But what if I get the job? How can I hide that from her?'

'We'll tell her about it when you've had the offer,' he says. 'Once the job's yours she won't make you give it up. We just have to make sure she doesn't find out before then. You don't want to end up working in a place like hers, do you?'

I shake my head.

'That's settled then. You're my boy. You need to follow in my footsteps, like I followed in your grandpa's. Memorise what's written on that piece of paper and then swallow it.' He notices his tiny cigarette has gone out, and makes a few attempts at trying to light it again. 'Don't look so worried,' he says, 'I'm only joking about swallowing the paper.'

I'm pretty sure I was looking worried, but none of it had anything to do with eating his note. It's what's written on the note that's giving me the fear.

'Borrow a suit from one of your cousins,' Dad says. 'I've got a couple in the cupboard, but they're too big for you. I'll give you a tie. Make sure you look smart.' He gives up on the remains of the tiny cigarette, and starts rolling another one. Then he tells me he's got some work to do in the garden, tells me to remind him to give me that note for school, taps the side of his nose, and leaves me sitting alone at the dining table in a severe state of hypertension.

None of this helps in any way with the brain freeze. In fact, it makes it about a hundred times worse. I find it almost impossible to concentrate on the problem of the iPad after that – all I can think about is how to get myself out of this horrifying interview, and I'm pretty sure that's all the back bit of my brain can think about too. I stumble around my kid room for a while, doodling on the wallpaper, trying to stop my mind racing, and checking my profile from time to time to see if there's any response from Elsie Green yet. Somehow, the iPad problem fighting with the interview problem results in me only being able to think about the Elsie Green situation, and I become convinced that she really is dead.

This leads on to a dark vision of me applying sticky labels to millions of whiskey bottles for the next fifty years, and eventually I can't take it any more and I have to get out of the house. Walking sometimes helps to get the ideas flowing, and it's the only strategy I haven't already tried over the weekend. I decide to walk out to the place where Elsie Green lives, and kill two birds with the one stone. If I can get a glimpse of her I can stop obsessing over the idea that she's gone belly up. And it's quite a long walk, so all the pavement pounding should get my mind turning over on the problems of the iPad and the interview. I check the computer one more time, see the familiar absence of the red dot, then grab my coat and put my desperate plan into action.

It turns out to be not too shoddy a plan, after all. I've only been walking for about ten minutes before I'm quite at peace with the whole interview thing. It starts to amaze me that I even got into a state about it. All I have to do is tell Mum it's been lined up, and then think of a way to smooth that out with Dad. He's right, there's no way Mum'll let me go through with it. Not before the exams. Maybe I can just tell him she found the bit of paper or something. Try convincing him it's really his fault for having written it all down in the first place. Then it'll just be a case of putting up with the Regular

Madness for a day or two, which is a small price to pay in the circumstances. And with that settled, and the Greensleeves situation currently in hand, my CPU will be free to get back to work on the question of the iPad again.

Here's how I lost Harry's iPad in the first place:

I'm in the dining hall one lunchtime, sitting with Sandy Hammil and a few randoms from his registration class who I don't really know. There's this one guy, Gary Crawford, whose dad works with my dad, so I know him a bit because of that. But the rest of them I don't know at all.

So this Gary guy, he starts going on about an attempt he's going to make on the school record for stuffing people into the wheelchair lift over in the new block. That's something we do sometimes, and Gary claims he's got a system to get fifteen in there. That seems pretty insane to me, but none of the randoms are saying much, just going along with it blindly. I think he probably has charisma or something like that. So eventually I say,

'Fifteen can't be done,' and they all kind of turn on me. 'I was in the last one,' I tell them. 'Eleven of us. If there had been one more I would've died. I'm still not sure I didn't die.'

'That plan was weak,' Gary says. 'Jennifer Campbell's diagram was old school. My schemata's totally porn. Look.'

It turns out his method of getting them all in there is as insane as his decision to go for fifteen in the first place. He's planning to put five face down on the floor, and then another five face down on top of them, at right angles. After that, all he has to do is squeeze five more round the walls, standing up, and he's got it made. According to him.

'What about the weight though?' I say. 'The rope was creaking with eleven. It won't hold fifteen.'

But he tells me the recommendation written on the lift is just for regulations.

'It'll take ten times what it says,' he insists. 'They have to do it like that.'

I don't disagree. It's designed to hold one person in a wheelchair, and one person helping them, and the weight it says is based on that. Obviously it takes more, since we managed to get eleven in there. But it was swinging quite a bit when we went up, and I'm certain the rope won't support fifteen.

'You should try for twelve,' I tell him. 'Twelve might work if you've got a new system. Fifteen is madness.'

'If I do twelve somebody will come along and break it,' he says. 'If I do fifteen, it'll stand forever. No one will ever beat fifteen.'

'Only because fifteen can't be done,' I say.

He puts his fork down on his plate then, and looks at me steadily.

'Do you want to put some money on it?' he asks.

I nod.

'Fifty quid,' he says. 'How about that?'

I don't have that kind of money, or anything like it, but I know he's got no chance of doing it, so I agree without even thinking it over.

'Let's see your money,' he says.

'Let's see yours.'

He goes into his pocket and takes out his wallet. A wallet! Then he opens that up and counts out five ten-pound notes. He holds them up in front of my face to show me.

'Where did you get all that?' I ask him.

'What are you talking about?' he says. 'Where did you get yours?'

'I haven't got any,' I say. 'Where would I get fifty quid?'

He looks at me sadly, as if I'm just a loser wasting his time.

'No money, no bet,' he says, and he puts the notes back in his wallet and folds it up. Then, just as he's tucking the wallet away in his pocket again, he sees Harry's iPad lying on top of my books, next to my plate of half-eaten gruel, and he looks at it approvingly.

'I'll take that,' he says. 'Put that up against my fifty and we've got a deal.'

So I put it up.

There was a point, about halfway through the wheelchair lift's journey, when I thought I'd won. I was standing up on the first floor, in amongst a crowd of pretty overexcited randoms, when there was this horrible crunching sound from the metal rope, and the sound of screaming from inside the car. It didn't stop moving though. A few seconds later it came into view and we could see two faces pressed hard up against the tiny window in the lift door, which was all steamed up with condensation. Then the doors opened and they all started spilling out.

Only Gary stayed in. He'd volunteered to be one of the bodies on the bottom layer, and we couldn't tell at first if he was dead or just milking it. He was just lying there, face down and unmoving. But then the rope made the cracking sound again, even louder than the first time, and then there was this big kind of bang. There was no doubt then about whether he was all right or not. He sprang out of the lift without even sitting up first, and landed on his feet out in the corridor. There were a few sparks and things, then another bang, and the lift car sort of tilted sideways and the lights inside went out. It didn't fall or anything, just hung like that, and when it was clear that nothing worse was going to happen some randoms started to cheer, and a bunch of them rushed towards Gary and started banging him on the back. He only seemed to have eyes for one person in the crowd though. Me. He walked straight up to me and grabbed my shirt.

'Give me the iPad,' he said, and I had no other option except to give it to him.

The lift is still hanging like that now. After it happened, this girl Irene, who's in a wheelchair, went to see Bailey with one of Gary's pals, and they told Bailey they were just going up in the lift when it went weird. And Bailey bought it. He didn't buy a new rope for the thing though. All the classes with pupils in them who need to use the lift have been moved down to the ground floor now, and Gary keeps boasting that his record will stand forever, because the lift will never get fixed. Every time I pass it on my way up or down the stairs I feel kind of sick, and I try my best to come up with a fail-safe trick to get Harry's iPad back off Gary.

But I never come up with anything.

12

For almost an hour, I sit on a wall across the road from Elsie Green's house, watching closely for a sign of life. The curtains are all open, and there's a car in the driveway, so I sit and watch for movement in the rooms at the front of the house. It took me ages to find the place. My friend Paul Glover is always going on about Elsie Green being his neighbour, so I found his house first and then studied all the name plates on the doors round about, looking for Green. It turns out she's not his neighbour at all. She lives down at the other end of the street, so far away I'm surprised he even knows she's there.

After about twenty minutes, a man comes out of the house and approaches the car, without closing the front door behind him. I lean forward on the wall, and start thinking I'm about to catch a glimpse of Elsie. I decide he must be driving her somewhere. He opens up the car and takes something off the passenger seat, then he carries it into the house. When he comes back he's on his own, and this time he closes the front door. Then he gets into the car, adjusts the mirror, reverses out onto the road, and drives away. I slump back into my original position on the wall, and start watching the windows again, excitement over.

I decide the man must be Elsie's dad. He didn't look much like a normal dad. He had a green jacket on, sort of furry, and his hair was kind of weird, all floppy and puffed up. I'm pretty certain that's the kind of dad Elsie would have. And the good thing is, he didn't look bereaved or in grief or anything like that. He wasn't crying and his eyes weren't rubbed red. He didn't even have a black tie on. So I take all that as a good sign. If only I could see her . . .

Half an hour later, there's still been no movement in any of the rooms. The car doesn't come back, and the front door stays closed. I'm just starting to drift off into thinking about the iPad, losing some of my concentration, when someone creeps up behind me and grabs me by the wrist.

'What are you doing?' a voice asks, and I almost jump out of my skin.

I turn round and there's an old man standing there, gripping me tightly, and staring at me with bulging eyes.

'I've been watching you,' he says. 'Get off my wall.'

I stand up but he still doesn't let go of my wrist. I'm pretty sure the way he's holding it is against my Human Rights. His hand feels horrible, all bony and cold, like a witch's hand.

'What are you doing here?' he asks me, and I try to tug my wrist out of his grip.

'I'm waiting for my friend,' I say.

'Which friend?'

'Paul Glover. He lives down there. He went back to get his jacket.'

'An hour ago?'

I try to think of some explanation for that, and then I just nod.

'I don't think so,' the old man says. 'I think you're casing the Green joint. You're part of a criminal syndicate.'

'A what?'

'A heist gang. I've been watching you. I know what's going on.'

'I'm only fifteen,' I tell him, and struggle with my wrist again. It feels like he's going to break it. There's no way that's not against my Human Rights.

'Fifteen!' he says, in that way, without laughing but sounding as if he is. I realise I should've used that myself. Right back when he said 'casing the Green joint'. Or I could have said: 'A criminal syndicate!' Or: 'A heist gang!' Now it's too late. He's beaten me to it. I really need to get on top of that thing.

He starts trying to drag me along the pavement and into his driveway. He's still on the other side of the wall, in his garden, and he grits his little teeth as he pushes and pulls. They look all thin and sharp, like white pins or something.

'Come on,' he says, 'I'm calling the police. You're waiting in here till they come. I've had enough of you.'

'I'm only waiting for my friend,' I tell him again, and tug and tug against his bony fingers. He screws his face up, exposing more of the little needle teeth, and then he starts to grunt. I reach out with my free hand and try to prise the bony witch fingers off my wrist.

'You're going down,' he tells me, and I bend one of the fingers back a little bit until he screams. I twist my wrist and pull, and suddenly I'm free.

'Murder!' he shouts, and I start running.

I run until I see a street turning off from the one I'm on, and then I nip down that one at a fair old speed. I keep doing the same thing every time a new street appears, and pretty soon I'm lost. I'm in a place I've never seen before, and I stop running for a minute and look about. Everything is quiet, and the little man is nowhere to be seen. I stand still, catching my breath and listening, but all I can hear are some birds tweeting and a couple of kids playing in a garden further up the street. When my heart stops bumping, and breathing doesn't seem so difficult any more, I realise I've escaped and start taking whichever turnings lead me back down the hill. I feel a bit annoyed that Operation Spot Elsie has been cut short, but it's balanced up by the relief of escaping the witch hand, and as I walk. I start to feel pretty certain that Elsie must be all right anyway, because of her dad not being in mourning or anything like that. I could probably have called time on the job as soon as I saw him, and saved myself another half hour of sitting on that wall, along with all the mad stuff that followed. But as it turns out, the little witch man has done me a favour anyway.

It turns out he's knocked all thoughts of the iPad out of my head, for the first time since I told Harry I'd get it back. And when I finally call it up again, I realise there's something new waiting for me there. A new thought. Not quite an idea, but the suggestion that I've been looking at the thing all wrong, trying to have the wrong idea. I've spent hour after hour wondering how to get the iPad back, forgetting that the iPad isn't really what's important. The iPad doesn't really matter. All that matters is getting Harry to tell Bailey he was in that fight. And the iPad is just one way to make him do that. But there must be others. Hundreds of others.

The thing is, I already had all the best ideas for getting the iPad back pretty soon after I lost it. And none of them worked. I offered Gary a double or quits bet, and he told me he didn't gamble.

'What about our bet?' I asked him.

'That wasn't gambling,' he said. 'That was a certainty.'

So I came up with all kinds of tricks for getting it back off him at school, but none of them were any good because he doesn't bring the iPad to school. He only uses it at home. And the only option that left me was breaking into his house, which isn't really my style.

No, getting round Harry will be a breeze compared to getting that thing back. So as soon as I see the steeple of the white church in the distance, and realise where I am again, I start walking at different speeds to get the frequency of my brainwaves locked into the ideal state, and then I give myself over to finding a new plan.

Nothing solid comes to me, but I know it will. That's just how things are. I'm an ideas man. It's only knowing what idea to have that sometimes muddles me up.

Dad's still out in the garden when I finally get home again. He's over in the corner, banging at something fragile-looking with a wooden mallet. I try to sneak in through the gate without him noticing me, but it doesn't work. Before I'm halfway down the path he turns round and holds the mallet up in the air, waving it about as if it's some kind of welcoming flag. Then he uses the other hand to call me over to where he is. He looks like a demented traffic cop who's totally lost the plot.

'I better get in,' I tell him. 'I'm feeling pretty tired.'

'Two minutes,' he says. 'I need to check something with you.'

I sigh and go a bit closer to where he's standing. There's all this broken stuff lying on the grass, the stuff he's been hitting with the mallet. I don't have a clue what any of it is. It looks a bit like hard cottage cheese.

'Come here,' he says, and he's not happy until I'm standing right up against him. Then he starts with the whispering again. 'Not a word to your mum about earlier,' he says. 'She's back home now. Remember, this is between us.'

I stare down at the smashed-up cottage cheese stuff.

'I think I have to tell her,' I say. 'It's giving me hypertension thinking up lies. It's going to spoil my performance in the interview.'

'Nonsense,' Dad says. 'You'll be fine. You can tell her when it's over.'

I shake my head. He looks at me and I stare at his mallet. 'What's all that stuff you've been breaking up?' I ask him.

'Just bits and pieces,' he says. 'Just getting things off my list.'

I notice what look like peanut shells lying in amongst the cottage cheese too. Then I look up at my dad, not quite at his eyes, just at his mouth or something.

'I think I'd better tell her,' I say, and I start walking back towards the path. He doesn't look very happy, but that can't be helped. Rather that than a lifetime of bottle-sticking.

'Don't, Jack,' he says, still in a sort of whisper. 'I'll owe you one.'

I avoid looking back and head into the house. I half expect him to follow me, but he doesn't. There's a moment of quiet and then the banging starts up again, the cottage cheese and peanuts taking the full brunt of his frustration.

I find Mum upstairs in her bedroom, sitting in front of the mirror twisting bits of rubber into her hair.

'Listen to that bloody noise,' she says. 'It's driving me crazy. What the hell's he doing out there anyway?'

'Working on his list,' I say. 'What's that you're putting in your hair?'

'Rubber things,' she says. 'I got them at the shops. I don't know if they'll work.'

'They look weird,' I tell her. 'Are you going to wear them outside?'

She tuts. 'You don't wear them. You put them in to make curls, then you take them out again.'

I nod. I pick one of them up off her table and look at it. It's kind of bendy. That's the sort of idea I'd like to come up with one day. Simple. I'll probably look online later to see who invented them in the first place. I might stick their picture in my book of role models. Successful ideas people.

'I need to tell you something about Dad,' I say, and Mum half turns away from the mirror, still keeping her eyes on the reflection of the blue thing she's twisting in.

'What's that?' she asks. 'What's he been doing now?'

And then it hits me. The zinger. My brain starts to tingle, and my fingers go all warm. I feel the familiar sensations before I'm even aware the idea is there, then the idea makes itself heard. Loud and clear. The brain freeze has thawed. I'm back in action.

'He . . .' I say, quickly trying to think up something different to tell her. 'I think he's gone a bit mad. I think he's smashing up cottage cheese on the lawn. You should probably call somebody.'

'It's been a long time coming,' Mum mutters, and I tell her I have to rush off for a minute.

I clatter down the stairs two and three at a time, and then haul the front door open. Dad hears it and turns round, kneeling on the grass with his mallet raised mid-attack. I walk quickly over to him.

'What did she say?' he whispers. 'Is it all off?'

I stay quiet for a moment and he lowers the hammer.

'I didn't tell her,' I say, and I watch the look of surprise appearing on his face. He tries to work out whether he can believe me or not, then he gets up on his feet and drops the mallet down into the grass.

'You didn't?' he says. 'Seriously?'

I nod, and he slaps me on the back.

'You're a good boy,' he says. 'The best. You'll love it in there once you get started. I know you will.'

'Maybe,' I say, severely doubting it. 'But you know when you told me you'd owe me one?'

'When?'

'When I said I had to tell Mum. You said you'd owe me one if I didn't.'

'Did I?' he says. He doesn't really look as if he believes me, but I power on.

'I think I might need your help now,' I tell him. 'I think I might need to call in that favour.'

He doesn't look very happy. He obviously didn't mean he

would owe me one at all. But he knows how easy it would be for me to go back upstairs and fill Mum in on all the finer details of the interview, so he sticks with it. He looks over his shoulder at his handiwork lying on the grass, then he turns back to face me.

'All right,' he says at last, bending down to pick up his mallet. 'What have I let myself in for this time? What is it you're after? Let's hear it.'

13

Half an hour later, I'm sitting in the car with my dad, a few doors down from Gary Crawford's house. The engine's turned off and I've explained the plan to Dad twice, once back at the house and once on the way here. He seems to understand it. He's not particularly happy about it, but he seems to understand it.

'Are you ready to go?' I ask him, and he holds up a hand to let me know he can't answer while his mouth's full. He chews noisily, continuing to hold up one finger of the hand, then he swallows.

'Just let me finish this,' he says. 'I need my vitamins.'

He insisted on stopping halfway there to buy a six-inch medium pan. He told me it was impossible for him to go into an operation like this on an empty stomach, and he tried to get me to have a pizza too. I told him I don't go into operations like this while I'm still digesting. It clouds the mind, and I tried to get him to see sense and wait till we were finished. But he told me it was each man to his own, and went ahead with his own way of doing things.

I sit and watch the windows steaming up, anxious just to get on with the thing. Then I start chattering to try and pass the time.

'Is it against your Human Rights if someone grabs hold of your wrist and won't let go?' I ask my dad.

He frowns while he decides which slice of pizza to pick up next. 'Depends why they did it, I suppose,' he says.

'What if you were just sitting on their wall?' I ask. 'What if you weren't doing anything wrong apart from that?'

'That seems fair enough,' he says. 'Nobody wants somebody sitting on their wall.'

'But you can't just grab them, can you? Surely that's against their Human Rights.'

'You're obsessed by human rights,' Dad tells me. 'Nobody had any human rights when I was young. Whose wall were you sitting on anyway?'

'Just an old guy's,' I say, and hold my wrist out to show him. 'Look, it's bruised. I think it might be sprained.'

He holds it up and then turns it over. He looks at the other side for a while and then turns it back. 'You're hallucinating,' he tells me. 'There's nothing wrong with it.' He rolls his own sleeve up and pushes his arm out in front of me. 'Look at that,' he says. 'That's a bruise.'

It certainly is. There's a big mark on his arm that looks like a full-scale haemorrhage.

'Can't even feel it,' he says. 'Once you're working in the bottling hall you'll get one of those nearly every day.'

He stuffs the last slice of pizza into his mouth, almost in one go, then he screws up his napkins, puts them into the box, and folds the box shut. He chews and swallows, chews and swallows, has quite a serious choking fit, throws the empty pizza box full of napkins onto the back seat of the car, and tells me he's ready to go.

'I'll just have a quick smoke first,' he says, and he rolls down the window and pulls out a cigarette. One that obviously wasn't made in his crazy new machine.

I think it was finally giving up on getting the iPad back that left my brain with the room it needed to come up with a solution. That's quite often how it works. Once I'd switched over to looking for a way to get round Harry there was no pressure on the thinking apparatus any more. It could just get on with its work. And that's exactly what it did.

So the first part of the plan is that I ring Gary's doorbell, while my dad stands off to the side, up against the wall of the house, facing out towards the road. We came up with that part together. If it's Gary who answers the door, I give a signal with my hand and Dad steps out beside me. If anyone else comes to the door, I ask if Gary's in, and when whoever it is goes to get him we swap places and my dad's standing there when Gary arrives.

It's Gary's mum who answers the bell. I ask if I can speak to Gary, and then hold my breath hoping she doesn't say he's out. She doesn't. She asks who I am and I tell her I'm Jack Dawson, then she shouts loudly to Gary there's someone at the door for him, and she walks away. Quickly, we make the switch, and I stand up against the wall, looking out at the road, listening intently to hear what's going on.

I hear some heavy footsteps coming down the hallway, and then I hear the door creaking open a little bit more. I imagine Gary must have been looking at the floor or something because he makes a sort of sniffing noise and doesn't seem to have noticed it's my dad standing there, then I hear the little note of surprise.

'Oh . . .' he says. 'I thought it was for me. Do you want my dad?'

'Probably,' Dad says. 'I've come to tell him about the wheelchair lift in the new block.'

Everything goes silent. I pretend to myself I can hear Gary swallowing. He creaks the door a bit, and then speaks very quietly.

'I didn't do anything,' he says.

Dad doesn't respond. I turn my head round to the side, still keeping it pushed up against the wall, and I see him just standing there.

'Is your dad in?' he finally asks Gary.

Gary doesn't say anything. I don't know if he's nodded, or shaken his head, or anything like that, but he doesn't speak.

'How will your dad take the news?' Dad asks, and I hear Gary saying it was an accident.

'I was just helping Irene up to the first floor,' he lies.

'You and fourteen others,' Dad replies. 'I found a copy of your diagram in Jack's room. It's clever. You'd make a good civil engineer if you weren't about to get expelled from school. But you probably shouldn't have signed it. That wasn't too bright.'

This is the only shaky part of the plan. If Gary asks to see the diagram at this point we're in a spot of hot water, since we don't really have one. If we did, I could've used it to get the iPad back weeks ago. But Gary's obviously in a bit of a blind panic, and he doesn't suspect for a minute that my dad's scamming him.

'What can I do?' Gary asks, and he's starting to sound quite scared.

'Jack says he lent you an iPad,' Dad says. 'And that you won't give it back.'

There are some more seconds of silence, and some more squeaking of the door. 'He said I could keep that,' Gary says.

'It's up to you,' my dad tells him. 'Jack's changed his mind, but you can either bring me the iPad or bring me your dad.'

I hold my breath. The door squeaks again. Then I hear Gary running down the hallway, and I hear his heavy feet clattering up the stairs. My dad takes a step back and turns towards me. I look at him and he lifts a thumb while still keeping his hands down by his sides. Then he takes a step towards the door again.

It's not long before I hear Gary thumping back down the stairs, and then I hear the glorious sound of the iPad changing hands.

'Can I have the diagram back?' Gary asks, and my dad says, 'Hmm . . .'

I hear some clicks as my dad turns on the iPad and plays about with it. I know he's got no idea what he's doing, and I hope he doesn't break the thing before I get it back.

'I think I'll keep the diagram for now,' he tells Gary. 'That way, if anything happens to Jack because of this, I can still show it to your dad.'

Gary stays quiet and my dad turns the iPad off again.

'Tell your dad I was asking for him anyway,' he says, and I hear Gary sort of tutting before he closes the door. I stay up against the wall until I'm sure he's gone, then I step away from it, feeling sharp little pains all over my back where the stones in the wall had been cutting into me.

'Let's go,' Dad whispers, and gives me a sort of disastrous low five, then we hurry back to the car and head for Harry's place.

14

After stopping for a twelve-inch crispy-thin on the way, with plenty of pineapples, I climb the stairs to Harry's room and knock on the door. There's no reply. I'm sure I can hear him moving about in there though, so I knock again.

Still nothing.

'It's Jack,' I shout, and I hear a soft groan coming from inside the room. I slip the iPad into my bag, then open the door myself and just walk in.

Harry's sitting over at his desk, playing a game of chess against himself, turning the board round to move a white piece then turning it back again to move a black one.

'Who's winning?' I ask him, and go and sit down on his kid's bed. He gives me a look as if to say, 'Very funny, I don't think!' and carries on playing. I make myself comfortable and look around his room for a while, then I drop the bombshell.

'I've brought you a present,' I say, and that gets his attention. The chess game is instantly abandoned. He jumps up from his desk mid-move, and comes across the room towards me.

'You've got the iPad?' he says. 'Seriously?'

I put a hand in my bag and then frown, as if it's not where I expected it to be. I search through the compartments, dipping in and out of them and making my frown deeper, then I lay my hand on it and look relieved. I draw it out as if I'm a magician bringing out a rabbit or something, and Harry lunges forward and pulls it out of my hands.

'That bastard Crawford better not have refurbished it,' he says. 'My stuff better still be on here.'

He slides his fingertip furiously around the screen, and I spend a few tense minutes just watching him like that, his face giving nothing away. Then, just when I'm starting to think I might hyperventilate, he punches a fist up into the air and shouts,

'Yes!' and I start breathing like I'm normal again.

'You did it, Jackdaw,' he says disbelievingly. 'It's all here. You really did it.'

For one awful moment I think he's about to kiss me, but then it passes.

'So we're on,' I say. 'You'll take the rap for the Chris Yates fight now?'

'First thing in the morning,' he replies. 'Just like I said I would. I'll be waiting outside Bailey's office before the bell rings for registration.'

I try to slow him down a bit.

'I've been thinking about that,' I say. 'We need to hold off until lunchtime. I haven't had time to square it all with Cyrus McCormack yet. I have to make sure he knows who he's supposed to have fought.'

Harry shakes his head. 'I'm not waiting,' he says. 'This is my chance now, Jack. I don't want to risk anybody else coming forward and spoiling it.'

I can't believe what I'm hearing. Two days ago we had all the time in the world apparently. Now he won't even let me get the plan straight.

'What the hell are you talking about?' I ask him. 'You said you were willing to wait as long as it took me to get the iPad back.'

'Only because I knew that would make you get it back,' he says. 'I was still going to Bailey first thing in the morning whether you brought it round tonight or not.'

'You bastard!' I say. 'I almost had a stroke trying to work out how to get it back for you. And I've landed myself with an interview at my dad's factory into the bargain.'

I lie back on his bed. My brain is whirring again. I need to find a way to convince him not to go to Bailey first thing in the morning. I need time to square the whole thing with Cyrus McCormack, or it'll turn into a complete disaster. And I don't even know Cyrus McCormack. I don't know the first thing about him.

A terrifying scene starts to take place behind my eyes. I see Bailey calling Cyrus into his office, and as Cyrus stands there Bailey points towards Harry, who's sitting over by the window.

'Is this the boy I caught you fighting with?' Bailey asks. 'Is this the boy you've been protecting?'

Cyrus looks over at Harry and wonders what's going on. He imagines Bailey must have been fed some false information by one of Yatesy's henchmen, and he wonders if he should just go along with it to save himself getting another beating, and to save the school trip. But then he thinks about the punishment

Harry will receive if he lies, and he shakes his head.

'It wasn't him,' Cyrus says, and the whole world crumbles to dust. Yatesy isn't off the hook, and my app lies in ruins. All my work has been for nothing. Harry has destroyed everything.

'You've got to give me till lunchtime,' I say to Harry. 'It won't work otherwise. Cyrus won't know what's going on and he'll tell Bailey it wasn't you. Then you won't have a hope in hell of getting to university, and you'll probably get suspended for lying.'

'It's a chance I'm willing to take,' he says. 'It's a bigger risk to leave it till later. Someone's bound to go to Bailey in the morning.'

'No they're not,' I say. 'No one's gone to him yet, have they? What difference will a couple of hours make? Just give me that.'

'I can't do it,' Harry says.

My brain whirrs. I search desperately for something, anything at all.

'How about this?' I say. 'What if I have a word with Yatesy tonight? Ask him to tell his people to spread the word that the school trip's safe. That someone's coming forward at lunchtime to take the blame. Then no one else has any reason to go to Bailey.'

He thinks about it. 'Could you do that?' he asks. 'Would that work?'

Of course it wouldn't.

'Of course it would,' I say. 'Yatesy's crew have managed to make sure no one's come forward so far. This would be pimps.'

He goes back to his desk, and sits down. He studies the pieces on the chessboard and moves one of them to a different square. Then he picks it up and moves it back again.

'Okay,' he says, 'I'll give you till lunchtime. But no longer than that.'

I feel a huge wave of relief washing over me. I stand up and reach out to slap him on the shoulders, but before I even make contact we both jump like we've been electrocuted. There's an almighty crash from downstairs that sounds like the ceiling falling in. We stare at each other in complete shock, and neither of us speak. My hand remains outstretched, but still not touching his shoulders. Harry's face is chalk-white. Then there's another almighty crash, and we hear the sound of a muffled voice, shouting loudly.

'Trucking banker!' it sounds like, or something like that, and we both head for the door and make a run for the stairs.

15

'Not a word,' my dad says. 'Agreed?'

We're back sitting outside our own house, with the car engine still running, and my dad pulls down the sun visor and opens up the mirror on it.

'Hell's teeth!' he says. He takes out a handkerchief and starts rubbing his face with it, then he spends a while fixing his hair and zips his jacket all the way up to his chin.

'Agreed?' he says again, and I nod. He nods too and turns the engine off. 'No point in worrying your mum,' he says. He looks in the mirror once more then folds the sun visor back into place, and we get out of the car and head inside.

Mum's sitting in the living room watching TV. Her hair looks curly now, and she doesn't have the twisty rubber things in it any more, but Dad doesn't seem to notice any difference.

'Where were you?' Mum asks. 'I was starting to get worried about you both.'

'We were round at Ray's,' Dad says, and Mum makes a pleased little noise.

'I didn't think of that,' she says. 'Did you have a nice time?'

'Cracking,' Dad lies.

'How about you, Jack?' Mum says. 'Did you have a nice time with Harry?'

I think of the moment where I asked Harry if he was ready to stand in for Yatesy and he told me he was. I just focus on that and try to forget about everything that happened afterwards, to keep the right kind of expression on my face.

'Brilliant,' I say, and Mum looks thrilled.

'Look at my two boys,' she says. 'Out there having adventures together.'

If only she knew the half of it.

When Harry and I got downstairs at Uncle Ray's place, my dad and Uncle Ray were both lying on the kitchen floor, and one of the wooden chairs was all smashed up, over by the sink. Uncle Ray had one hand in my dad's hair, and the other beneath his chin, trying to push my dad's face away. My dad had both hands on Uncle Ray's collar, and his feet were kicking along the floor at Uncle Ray's feet and shins. My dad's nose was bleeding all over the place, and the cut on Uncle Ray's chin from the other day, which had looked a lot better when we arrived earlier, was bleeding onto his shirt again, and they were both making strange grunting noises and swearing a lot.

'Dad!' Harry shouted, and they looked round and saw us standing there, and almost at once the struggling stopped. Uncle Ray tried to smile, which looked quite strange under the circumstances, and then he glanced at my dad very briefly.

'Just a minor tussle,' he said. 'Just a bit of fun, boys. I imagine you were doing pretty much the same thing upstairs.'

Even my dad looked baffled, but he got to his feet along with Uncle Ray, and Uncle Ray put an arm round my dad's shoulders and pulled him close while they both stood facing us.

'So that's how you do The Buckle,' Uncle Ray said to Dad. 'It's an old wrestling move,' he told us. 'Your dad thought it went differently, Jack, but he was thinking of The Double Slam.'

'You're a moron, Dad,' Harry said, and he left the room and headed upstairs.

'Go and borrow a suit from Harry,' my dad said. 'For the interview. Then we're leaving.'

I hurried after Harry and while I was up there some more shouting started, and there were another couple of bangs. But when I got back down my dad was standing at the door, holding it open, and signalling to me to get outside.

'Don't be a stranger, Jackdaw,' Uncle Ray shouted from the kitchen, and I told him I wouldn't.

Dad grabbed the suit off me and pushed me outside. Then he threw the suit onto the back seat of the car and reversed out of the driveway without even checking to see if there was anything coming, the tyres screeching when we reached the road.

He drove like a maniac until we had to stop at a set of traffic lights, then he rolled the window down and stuck his head outside, shouting, 'You're a madman, Ray. You're totally insane.'

Given the fact that we were about three streets away by then, I doubted if Uncle Ray could hear him, but I didn't say anything about that to my dad.

When the lights turned green again he started slamming the steering wheel with the palms of his hands as he drove away.

'That bampot!' he said through gritted teeth, and then he turned to me. 'Sorry, Jack,' he said. 'That was just . . .' and then he made a kind of roaring sound. 'I'm okay,' he said, 'I'm okay. Calm down, Andy. Get a grip on it.' He wiped his nose with the back of a hand, and then looked down to see all the blood there. 'Buggeration,' he said, and he started doing that thing to the steering wheel again for a little while.

We were almost all the way home before he'd calmed down enough to stop being mental. He pulled in at the side of the road on the street before our own, and he took some deep breaths, saying, 'I'm okay,' over and over again. He tipped his seat back a bit, stretching out on it, and he started rolling up one of his little cigarettes.

'I can't believe that idiot,' he said, while he spread the tobacco out on the little piece of paper. 'He's out of his mind. He seems to think we're still about ten years old. Fighting! Two grown men!'

He licked the bit of cigarette paper to make it sticky, and rolled it up tight.

'Not a word about any of this to your mum,' he said. 'She'd go through the roof.'

'What were you fighting about anyway?' I asked him.

He shook his head. 'Nothing,' he said. 'I told him that black eye was his own fault for refusing to stop singing. Something like that. He told me his singing brings joy to millions, lights up people's lives. So I asked him why he had the black eye if that was the case. Then he asked me if I wanted to "go at it". Go at it! Heavenly Christ. He's like a big retarded kid. He's a bampot.'

'Does that mean we won't be seeing him again?' I asked, and my dad hunted around in his pockets for his lighter.

'It'll all blow over in a couple of days,' he said. He lit up his cigarette and started smoking it, rolling the window down slightly. 'Ray's probably forgotten about it already.'

We sat there without saying anything else until the cigarette was almost gone, and my dad dropped it out the window. Then he fixed his seat back up, and drove round the corner to our own place.

'Not a word,' he said, when we pulled into the driveway. 'Agreed?'

You know the rest . . .

Upstairs, I lie on my bed for a while, staring at the ceiling with a brain that feels burnt and tight after all the thinking it's done over the weekend. It occurs to me I should go and look to see if Cyrus McCormack has a profile online, and just as I have that thought I also remember I could check for Elsie's red dot while I'm there. I imagine myself getting up off the bed to do it, but in reality I just keep lying there. I hear my dad coming upstairs and going into the bathroom, then I hear him unzipping his jacket and the tap being turned on hard. I listen to him splashing about noisily, and just keep staring up at the ceiling.

Eventually, though, I manage to drag myself off the bed and over to the computer. It isn't really worth the effort. There's still no red dot from Elsie, and Cyrus doesn't seem to have a profile. If he does, I certainly can't find it. And on top of all that, I have another message from Drew Thornton to contend with.

'Hi, Jackdaw,' it says. 'Hope you had a good weekend. What did you get up to? I went to the Warcraft fair in Forbidden Planet. See you tomorrow. Drew.'

I let my finger hover over the mouse for a while, with the cursor sitting on the button to delete Drew as a friend. I don't have the heart to go through with it though. Instead I open up a reply box and start typing.

'Hey, Drew,' I write. 'The Warcraft fair sounds awesome. I just did the usual stuff. Got attacked by an old witch man while I was trying to work out whether Elsie Green had killed herself or not, and consigned myself to a life of sticking labels onto whiskey bottles for the next fifty-odd years. I scammed my cousin's iPad back from Gary Crawford, and single-handedly saved the school trip by convincing my cousin to stand in for Chris Yates. Then my dad had a punch-up with his brother about a punch-up his brother had had with someone else. Just the usual boring stuff. Take it easy, Jack.'

I don't have any intention of sending it, but I sit staring at it for a while, trying to take it all in. I find myself starting to wish I could just pay attention in class, and study properly for the exams. Life would be a lot simpler. I add in another bit after the bit about Elsie killing herself that says 'over her love for you', then I backspace most of it away and write a proper reply.

'Hey, Drew,' it says. 'Hope you enjoyed that Warcraft fair. My weekend was good. Mostly just vegging out at my cousin's. Beat him at chess. School tomorrow – bad news. Jackdaw.'

I check it over and click on send, and just as it disappears there's a knock on my door. I get up from my desk and it's my dad with Harry's suit.

'You left this in the car,' he says, and he comes into the room and closes the door behind him. 'Everything good?' he asks, and I tell him it is, even though I'm not sure what he's talking about. He's changed his shirt, and his hair is back to normal now. There are no signs of blood left around his nose.

'Good,' he says, then he puts a hand in his back pocket. 'I forgot to give you this earlier,' he tells me, and holds out a piece of paper. I take it and try to work out what it is. It doesn't make any sense to me.

'Is it a form?' I ask him.

'An application form,' he says. 'For the job. Fill it in and I'll come and get it before I go to bed. I'll hand it in at the office in the morning.'

I look the thing over. 'It asks about qualifications and experience and stuff,' I say. 'What will I put there?'

'Don't worry about it,' he tells me. 'It's just so they know who you are. Regulations. Just put in whatever you think. Make sure it's neat.'

He disappears and leaves me to it, and I put the form on my desk and go back to sit on my bed. I look from the form to the suit, and then from the suit back to the form again. It doesn't make me feel good, and I don't see a particularly restful night ahead.

16

For the first time in my life, I get to school as early as I possibly can, and stand near the gates waiting for Cyrus McCormack to come in. I see Drew Thornton quite early on and hide behind a bin before he sees me. I watch carefully as he wanders down to the playground and disappears into the crowd, lost in a world of his own, probably still dreaming about his Warcraft fair. Then I decide to stay behind the bin for the time being. There are quite a few people I'd rather not have to talk to, and I tick them off as they come in: Gary Crawford, my cousin Harry, Chris Yates. All the dominoes from the middle of my sequence. But by the time the bell rings for registration, there's still no sign of Cyrus, the domino that will set the whole thing in motion, and there's no sign of the one it's all leading up to: Elsie Green. I give it a few more minutes, watching latecomers and strays hurrying through the gate with their bed hair still on, then I decide Cyrus and Elsie must have arrived at school before I got there, and head for my class.

After registration it's a double boredom of History, with Sergeant Monahan. The first bit zips by in quite a spritely fashion because it turns out we had homework, and I've forgotten to do it. Monahan powers up the proceedings by choosing randoms in no particular order and getting them to read out what they've written for the benefit of the whole class. Waiting on my name to be shouted gets my adrenalin pumping quite sufficiently, and the time seems to pass at a rate of knots. I'm only saved by the fact that Eric Beadle's name gets called before mine, and he very clearly hasn't applied himself over the weekend either. He makes an admirable attempt at putting something together while he talks, but Monahan sees through it and hauls Eric along the corridor to see Bailey, the headmaster, leaving me free to copy Elaine Cochrane's work while he's gone, and to mix it up with some of what I've already heard while I was waiting for my name to come out of the hat.

From there on in, though, the time drags like a week at my aunt Margaret's place. Monahan uploads terabytes of data about an ancient guy who was found in a muddy bog, perfectly preserved. It all sounds quite gruesome, from what I manage to catch. Something about seeds he'd eaten being found in his stomach, and something about a rope tied around his neck. Something about him being over a thousand years old. Not the sort of thing you want to be thinking about first thing in the morning. Monahan even shows us a picture at one point, but I don't look at it. I think there's probably some charity or organisation I could contact to get him put on a list of some kind, for attempting to psychologically damage minors.

I spend a good part of the rest of the lesson thinking about that, and it helps the time to pass less painfully.

During break time, I run all over the school trying to track Cyrus down. I come across people who tell me they've seen him but can't remember when, and others who tell me exactly where he is, and then he turns out not to be there. When the break ends I'm beginning to get frantic, and I move amongst the crowds in the corridors hoping desperately to catch a glimpse of him.

I don't.

As the corridors start to empty I realise I'm so far away from Baldy Baine's class I'm going to have to sprint to make it in time, so I don't go to Baldy Baine's class at all. Instead I spend the next double wandering from classroom to classroom, peeking into each one through the little pane of glass in the door, trying to see if Cyrus is in there.

I had no idea that there were so many classrooms in the school before. There must be like a thousand or something. But I don't see Cyrus in any of them. Or Elsie Green. I see Drew Thornton, Gary Crawford, my cousin Harry and Chris Yates. And quite a few randoms see me, and most of them give me the finger. But there are areas down the left-hand side and along the back wall in each class that I can't see, so I assume Cyrus and Elsie must be in one of those spots.

By the time the lunch bell rings, I've already got a new strategy up and running. I'm standing at the door to the dining hall, knowing Cyrus and Elsie aren't already in there, ready to grab them as soon as they pass. The thing is though, that's when the hunger hits me. I skipped breakfast to get into school as early as I did, and all the miles I've covered between then and now have used up so many calories I suddenly feel as if

I'm about to pass out. I'd even be willing to share the bog man's stomach seeds with him, given half a chance, and all I can do is run into the dining hall on a pair of rubber legs, and start eating things off my tray before I've even found a table.

It's not until Sandy Hammil comes and sits down beside me, and I'm bolting the last few spoonfuls of my raspberry-flavoured jelly water, that I start to feel human again.

I grab a few chips off Sandy's plate and look up to find the room has finally stopped spinning. I take a deep breath and sit back in my seat, exhausted. Then I close my eyes.

'Were you off this morning?' Sandy asks, and I shake my head. 'But you weren't in Baine's class,' he says.

I wonder if he thinks this is news to me. Maybe he thinks I pay so little attention in school I was sitting somewhere else entirely, thinking I was in Baine's class.

'I had some things to take care of,' I tell him, finally opening my eyes. 'This Elsie Green thing is killing me.'

'You should have been in class,' Sandy says. 'Everything we're getting now is going to be in the exams.'

I grab a few more chips off his plate and tell him the exams are dead to me.

'My dad's set up an interview for me first thing in the morning,' I say. 'If I can't make this app work I'll be sticking labels on bottles before the exams even start.'

He looks shocked. 'I told you that would happen,' he says. 'I kept telling you to start paying attention in class.'

But I tell him that paying attention isn't all it's cracked up to be. 'You should've heard what Monahan was spouting this morning,' I say. 'Paying attention to that kind of stuff could seriously damage your health.'

'What kind of stuff?' he asks.

'I don't know. I wasn't listening. But it had something to do with a dead guy, all wrinkled up and buried in wet clay.'

'You're a maniac,' Sandy says. 'Anyway, where were you at the weekend? I thought you said you were coming round.'

I have no memory of saying that, but I suppose I must have, so I apologise.

'I had to deal with the Elsie Complications,' I say. 'I spent all weekend convincing my cousin Harry to take the rap for that fight Chris Yates was in. And ever since then I've been trying to find Cyrus McCormack, to square the story with him.'

Sandy forks a piece of beef, considers it for a moment, then decides against it.

'Cyrus's sitting behind you,' he says, and I spin round in my seat.

'Where?' I ask.

'Over at the windows. Next to John Walker.'

I check it out, and Sandy's absolutely right. Cyrus is sitting there quite happily, shovelling food into his mouth, and banging away to John Walker about something that seems to be boring John rigid.

'I'll be back in five minutes,' I tell Sandy, getting up from my chair. But the truth is, I'm not going anywhere. Before I can even get properly to my feet someone else sits down at our table, in the chair directly opposite mine. There's no 'Hello,' or 'Is anyone else sitting here?' or anything like that. Not even a friendly nod. All they say is,

'I need to talk to you, Jack. Right now.'

And I lower myself back into my seat again. It's Elsie Green.

I don't know if she'd have waited for Sandy to leave even if he'd tried to. I don't think she even notices he's there. She just pushes her tray off to the side a bit, stabbing at bits of potato with a strange-looking fork, and then launches straight into her bizarre madness.

'Do you have a sore stomach, Jack?' she asks me. 'Just about there?'

And she touches her own stomach quite high up and stares at me without blinking.

'I'm expecting to get one quite soon,' I say. 'I just ate the leather beef and the jelly water.'

'Don't be flippant,' she tells me. 'It doesn't suit you.'

I eyeball Sandy and he looks kind of afraid and fascinated at the same time. He's staring at Elsie's strange hat with the feather in it, and at her weird velvet cape thing.

'Does it feel tight?' she asks me.

I consider my stomach. It just feels normal.

'I don't think so,' I say. 'It feels fine.'

Even by her standards this is starting to seem like bonkers behaviour. She's never come and spoken to me in her life before, and now this. I brace myself and get ready to ask why she hasn't friended my profile yet.

'Are you feeling sick?' she says, and Sandy laughs a little bit.

'It's lunch time in the dining hall,' he says. 'Everyone is feeling sick.'

But Elsie doesn't even seem to notice he's spoken.

'I think I know what's been going on,' she says. 'I just want to hear it from your own lips, Jack. Be honest with me – does the project you want me to work on even exist?'

I suddenly feel as if I've been punched. 'Of course it does,' I say, probably a bit too loudly. 'Why? Who told you it doesn't?'

'Just the wind,' she says. 'Just the leaves in the trees. Even what you did to spoil my courtship with Stephen makes sense to me now.'

The *leaves* in the *trees*?

I steal a glance at Sandy and he gives me the crossed eyes and sticks his tongue out the side of his mouth.

'What are you talking about, Elsie?' I ask. 'I don't think I'm following any of this.'

'Yes you are,' she tells me. 'I saw you yesterday, Jack. I saw you beneath my window waiting to begin your song. Such devotion.' She turns to Sandy as if they've been chatting away all along, and as if she hasn't been continually blanking him. 'He was there for hours,' she says, and Sandy lifts his eyebrows away up into his hair.

'One hour,' I say. 'Even less than one hour. And—'

She holds a hand up to stop me, and Sandy looks as if he's starting to enjoy this. The bastard.

'I got the message you sent me too,' she says. 'The friend request. And a friend told me about your scene with Drew Thornton in the corridor on Friday afternoon. They said you looked quite incensed. So I want to give you the chance of explaining what's going on.'

'Nothing's going on,' I tell her. 'Well, quite a lot's going on, really. Everything's under control, though. I'm just working away on—'

I stop, suddenly realising Sandy doesn't know anything

about Operation Naked Drew, and that's exactly how I want to keep it. 'I'm just working away on . . . your request,' I say. 'It's become a bit complicated, but it's going to happen, Elsie. No question.'

'Such selflessness,' she whispers. 'Isn't love a strange taskmaster?' she says to Sandy. 'The very thing that will break Jack's heart, he's willing to do in the service of my happiness.' She turns back to me. 'Nothing can ever come of this longing I've awakened in you,' she says. 'I hope you understand that. You know how deeply devoted I am to Drew.'

'Will you still help me with my programming, though?' I ask her. 'If I manage to do the Drew thing for you?'

She looks at me with what I can only imagine she thinks is extreme pity. 'If you feel the need to continue that tenuous connection between us, then I'll do it,' she says. 'As long as you fulfil your promise.'

'Thanks, Elsie,' I say, and a massive sense of relief wells up in me. I can't say I've got any idea what she's been talking about, but I was starting to get scared she might cancel the Objective C agreement. After everything.

She organises her tray and gets to her feet, the bizarre cape thing swishing about and covering Sandy's face for a minute. Then, just as he pushes it out of the way, she leans across the table, and gives me this terrifying kiss on the cheek.

'Be brave,' she whispers, then she turns to Sandy. 'Look after him,' she says, and as she floats away the first year girls who passed me in the corridor last time I was talking to Elsie walk past again.

'I told you she was your girlfriend,' the squeaky-voiced one says, and Sandy starts having the time of his life. He looks as if he's about to burst. He tries to speak and has to stop three or four times before he finally gets it out.

'You certainly were busy at the weekend,' he says. 'Let's hear your song then, Jackdaw. Did you write it yourself?'

He starts laughing like a maniac, and I tell him to give it a rest, although I'm not sure he can even hear me over the noise he's making.

'I wasn't anywhere near her window,' I say. 'I was away across the road. Let me tell you what really happened.'

But while he's still laughing, and while I'm starting to get pretty angry at him, somebody or something starts tugging at my sleeve and I try to push it away without looking round.

'Jackdaw,' a voice is saying. 'Jack.'

'Get a grip on yourself, Sandy,' I say, still pushing away the thing that's tugging at my arm. Sandy calms down a bit, and I consider how to explain to him what's been going on without having to go into the exact details of Operation Naked Drew. But the tugging on my sleeve and the chattering in my ear are making it impossible to think, and I finally turn round to see my cousin Harry standing there.

'It's the end of the lunch break,' he tells me.

'Thanks for the update, Harry,' I snap. 'Stop raping me, will you? I'm trying to sort something out here.'

'But it's the end of the lunch break,' Harry says again. 'I'm going to Bailey's office now.'

And he lets go of my sleeve, and starts walking away. Suddenly, I'm sweating. I spin round in my chair to look for Cyrus McCormack and I can't see him any more. The table where he was sitting before is empty now, and I look desperately round the dining hall, but there's no sign of him anywhere. All I can see is my cousin Harry gradually fading into the crowd, and all I can hear is the sound of Sandy still laughing.

'Harry!' I shout. 'Wait! Nothing's been sorted yet.'

He doesn't even turn round. I get up from the table and look quickly at Sandy.

'Wait till Harky hears about that kiss,' he says. 'And Davie Brown.'

'Don't tell anybody anything,' I hiss.

'I won't need to,' Sandy laughs. 'The leaves will tell them. And the wind.'

I've got two disasters on my hands at once, and I grip onto the table, turning back and forward between Harry, who's getting closer and closer to the dining hall door, and Sandy, who's quite hysterical, and getting purple in the face.

'I'll be back in a minute,' I tell Sandy. 'I'll clear the whole thing up. Not a word to anybody, I mean it.'

'I'll await your return with infinite devotion,' he laughs again, and I give him a vicious look. Then I start pushing my way through the throng of disgruntled diners, and make a beeline for my demented cousin, in an attempt to stop him bringing the whole thing to the ground.

Options: you need to keep them open in an emergency. So while I'm charging towards Harry, I make sure to ask various randoms if they saw which way Cyrus went. While I'm still in the dining hall most of them point towards the dining hall doors, which isn't too much of a surprise. Once I'm out in the corridor they either point to the main doors or they point out into the playground. I keep my eye fixed on Harry as he speed-walks along the corridor, and when I reach the main doors I have to make my choice. If I nip out into the playground and find Cyrus it doesn't matter what Harry does. As long as I can fill Cyrus in with what's happening the whole thing will run like clockwork. But if I dive out there and still haven't managed to lay my hands on Cyrus before Bailey sends for him, everything could quite easily go up in smoke. So I decide the safest option is to head Harry off first, in case Cyrus proves to be as elusive as he's been all morning, and I double my speed to make sure I reach Harry before he's at the end of the corridor. Then I grab him by the arm just as he's about to push the doors open and head into the open area where Bailey's office is.

'Quit it!' Harry says, trying to shake me off.

'Slow down, then,' I tell him. 'I still need to put a few things in place.'

'I don't care,' he says. 'You had your chance. Lunchtime, we said. I kept up my end.'

'But I only need five minutes,' I say, and I get in front of him and stand between him and the double doors. He keeps trying to lunge past me, but I manage to anticipate his moves and block his path. 'I couldn't find Cyrus this morning, Harry. I've only just managed to track him down. He's right out there in the playground. I only need five minutes to have a quick word with him.'

'Go and do it then,' Harry says, and he lunges for the door again. I get to him just in time and push him backwards, and he kind of staggers.

'Stop being a knob,' he says, and I get a bit wound up. Then I realise if this starts to look like a fight we'll have a crowd round us before we know what's happening, and Bailey will come tanking out of his office all fired up. Harry could get suspended without needing to take part in my scheme, and I'll probably get expelled.

I do what I can to calm it down.

'Listen,' I say, 'everything's under control. Let's go and find Cyrus. Five minutes, that's all. Then you're on a ticket to university. What's the point in risking it all?'

He goes kind of loose; his arms hang by his sides. 'Did you sort everything out with Chris Yates?' he asks. 'Is he putting the word round?'

'Of course,' I lie. 'That's all taken care of. All we have to do is let Cyrus get a good look at your face, let him commit it to memory, and then it's game on.'

He screws his mouth up and then looks over his shoulder, back along the corridor. 'Where is he?' he asks.

'Just out there,' I say. 'Just out the main doors.'

'Move it then,' Harry says, and I give him a good hard push and we head back the way we came.

I start thinking Cyrus maybe has the ability to teleport. Or turn invisible whenever he wants. Trying to find him starts out like a rerun of the morning's fiasco. Everyone's directions lead to nothing, and Harry is soon getting jumpy and ready to make a dash for Bailey's office before the bell rings for the end of lunch. Then, just when I'm trying to work out how to head him off again, somebody tells us Cyrus is round the back of the old building, down near the bins, so we follow their directions and there he is, standing with a group of weirdos all pointing their phones together in the middle of a circle. When we get closer it looks like they're playing some kind of geeky game, all shouting and frothing at the mouth. Cyrus is wiggling his phone about with the rest of them, and we stand back and watch until Cyrus groans loudly and pulls his phone out of the circle. He holds it up and looks at the screen, pushing some buttons, while the rest of them keep wiggling and foaming, and we take a few steps closer to him.

'Cyrus!' I say, and he looks up then looks back at his phone again. 'We need to talk.' He shakes his head, so I move closer until I'm standing right beside him. I look at his phone and there's a little cartoon duck on it, moving about. 'This is my cousin Harry,' I say.

'So what?' Cyrus shrugs. 'I don't even know who *you* are.'

'I'm The Jackdaw,' I tell him, and he starts laughing. Some of the phone goons start laughing too.

'More like The Sparrow,' Cyrus says, and the phone junkies crease up. I laugh a little bit too, just to keep him sweet. I can already understand why Chris Yates found it necessary to lay into him. Even though Chris was on a final warning. But I chuckle along with the witticism, and nod as if Cyrus is some kind of super-brain.

'We want to talk to you about that moron Chris Yates,' I say. That wakes him up. Suddenly he's all ears, and I ask him to step away from his retard gang, so we can talk properly, although I don't call them his retard gang to his face.

Harry stands fidgeting with his watch strap while I lay the whole thing out for Cyrus. I tell him all he really needs to do is remember Harry's face, and give a quick nod when Bailey asks if this is who he was fighting.

'He might not even ask you,' I say. 'It's just a precaution.'

I tell him how it will save the school trip, and I explain all about what it will mean to Harry. How it will sort things out between him and his dad. How it will get him into university.

I give it my all. It make it so's it couldn't be simpler, or easier, or less skin off Cyrus's nose. I lay it all out in less than a couple of minutes. Done and dusted.

And Cyrus isn't having any of it.

17

I spend most of the night lying awake, staring into the darkness. There's a point early on where I start to drift off, when I see a big orange shape and hear the dream voices chattering, but then my door opens and my dad shoves his head into the room.

'You awake, Jack?' he says, and I make a noise to let him know I'm probably not. He takes it to mean I've just been lying there waiting for someone to chat to, and he comes in and stands beside my bed.

'Good luck for the morning, pal,' he says. 'I've brought you a tie.' He holds it up in the darkness but I can't see anything. 'Don't worry about tomorrow.' he says. 'I spoke to Frank Carberry this morning and he says the job's yours. The interview is just to keep things above board.'

Something to really help me fall asleep without a care.

'Is the suit in good shape?' Dad asks. 'I could run an iron over it before I go to bed.'

I make another kind of sleeping noise and then mumble that it's fine. He goes over and puts the light on, just about taking my eyes out, then he picks the suit up off the back of the chair. He hums a bit while he's holding it up to inspect it.

'Looks okay,' he says, then he puts it back where it was, in a bit more of a crumpled state, and lays the tie on top of it.

'Come in and see me when the interview's over,' he tells me. 'I'll be in the bottling hall. Let me know how it went.'

'All right,' I say, and he turns the light out again and leaves me to spend some productive hours going over and over the mess I've got myself into.

I think for a long time about Cyrus, wondering what it matters to him whether he tells Bailey he fought Yatesy or Harry. I lie there wide awake, trying to convince him in my head to say it was Harry after all.

He seemed a little bit insane in the playground when I was trying to get him to do just that.

'Yatesy's going down for this,' he kept saying. 'I'll make sure of it.'

'But why?' I asked him.

'Because he ruined my life. And he's going to pay for it. Guaranteed.'

'But think of how you'd be helping Harry out.'

'Who the hell is Harry?' Cyrus asked, and I pointed towards him. 'Who the hell *is* he, though?'

'He's my cousin.'

'But who the hell are *you*? I don't know either of you. And you'd better not mess this up for me. If either of you go to Bailey and tell him I fought this guy, I'll go straight there and tell him it's a lie. I won't even wait to see if Bailey bothers to ask me.'

Harry made a strange little noise, but I didn't dare look at him.

'In fact,' Cyrus said, 'I might even go to Bailey now and tell him what you said to me. How would you like that?'

'Your word against ours,' I said. 'I'll tell him it's a blackmail.'

Cyrus looked at his phone for a minute and pressed a few buttons on it. It started making a noise and he pressed a few more buttons, then he held it out to us. There was a big ugly grin on his face. The phone was playing back the conversation we'd just had.

'Get lost, Sparrow,' he said, and he went back to his weirdo little gang who all stared at us as we walked away. By the time the bell rang for the end of lunch break, Harry and I were back round the front of the school and I hadn't spoken a word to him.

'Don't bug me again, Jack,' he said. 'I've had it with you.'

'Me?' I said. 'What did I do? All I'm trying to do is help.'

'You're an idiot,' he told me. 'If you'd let me go and see Bailey when I wanted, it might have worked out. He might not even have asked Cyrus.'

'But you heard what Cyrus told us. He'd have gone to Bailey anyway and said it wasn't you.'

'Maybe,' Harry replied. 'But maybe not. And he wouldn't have had the evidence you've just given him. You're a moron. We're finished.'

He walked away and I stood about for a while trying to work out where I was and where I was supposed to be. I finally worked out I had French and made my way there at a snail's pace. And, just when I thought things couldn't get any worse, I walked into the class to hear them all humming the tune 'Greensleeves' under their breaths, while a few of them tried to make kissing noises.

'Silence!' the teacher shouted, and I decided I was going to kill Sandy Hammil.

* * *

In the early hours of the morning, when the room is getting brighter, I start to see the big orange shape and hear the chattering of dream voices again. I stop thinking about Cyrus and my body goes soft and light. Then the bedroom door opens. Then my dad comes and stands at the side of the bed again.

'I'm away now,' he says. 'Don't sleep in.'

Not much chance of that.

'What time is it?' I ask him.

'Quarter to seven.'

'What time is the interview?'

'Half nine.'

'I think I'll be all right,' I say, and he rubs the quilt up near my shoulder, then he leaves the room and goes to work.

That's the last I see of the big orange shape for one night. The room gets brighter and brighter, and I just lie with my eyes open taking part in an imaginary version of my interview. The Frank Carberry guy sits behind a desk, and I sit on the other side, trussed up in Harry's suit.

'You won't be handling bottles straight away,' the Carberry guy tells me. 'We'll start you off on label licking. You'll hand the labels to a more experienced random and they'll stick them on. It's hard to get them straight at first. All right?'

'What if my tongue gets all squeaky?' I ask him.

'No problem,' he says. 'We've got stuff for that. A pump-action spray. But we can start you first thing in the morning. Sound good?'

I tell him I've got double History, and he tells me he'll write me a note. Then he brings out this piece of paper for me to sign that says I'll stay on for fifty years, and won't drink any of the whiskey from the broken-glass oil drums.

Maybe I am sleeping a bit, after all. Either that or I'm having a full-scale mental collapse. I hear the front door slam, meaning Mum has left for work now too, and I decide I can't take any more of the fake Frank Carberry and I head along the hallway for a shower. Then I get myself ready.

Harry's suit looks completely bonkers when I put it on. I don't know where he ever wore it, but it's the stupidest thing I've ever seen. It looks as if it's made out of tinfoil, all silver and shiny, and I'm not even sure it fits me. I've put on the white school shirt I never wear, and I have a go at fixing up my dad's tie. It's quite a wide thing, sort of woolly and green, and I don't really know if this is a good way to look when I check it all out in the mirror. I don't think so. I know you're supposed to look kind of insane when you go for an interview, but I don't know if this is too much insane or not. I should've had a trial run in front of my dad last night.

I take his big tie off and try wearing my school one instead. Can you do that? At least it's quite narrow, but maybe it's just as crazy as wearing the whole school uniform. I wonder if I need a tie at all. Eventually I decide to put the green one back on, and sit over at my desk, exhausted. I can't carry on like this. I need to think of a way round the whole Cyrus situation. Maybe I need another plan entirely. Maybe I need to trace my line of dominoes all the way back to where it went wrong, and start over from there again. Maybe there's a different way to get Drew Thornton naked. Maybe Yatesy was the wrong path to go down in the first place.

I get myself a bit fired up on that, and it's enough to give me the energy to contemplate heading downstairs for breakfast. Should I have put my suit on after my breakfast? What if I drop some cereal onto the tinfoil suit? I think about putting my pyjamas back on, but I couldn't bear to go through the whole tie business again. I'd need to look in the mirror to get it right, and my plan now is to avoid mirrors until the interview is over. That way I can just pretend I look all right.

I put my shoes on and rub them with the corner of my quilt, then I pick up my phone and make a break for the kitchen, only to find my mum sitting waiting at the bottom of the stairs.

'Looking sharp this morning, Jack,' she says. 'Looking very sharp indeed.'

18

One time, I saw this bit in a comic where a character got caught between two decisions, and he froze at that point in time forever. He wasn't sure which decision to go with, and he made an attempt to do them both at once, and that was supposed to be why he got caught there. That's exactly how I feel when I get to about three-quarters of the way down the stairs, and see Mum sitting there. I can't decide whether to carry on going down, or to turn round and run back up to my room and lock the door. So I just freeze on the step, and stand there trying to smile.

'Hello,' I say eventually, and I think Mum almost laughs.

'Good morning,' she says.

My head is completely empty. I can't think of anything. She sits there next to the telephone, looking at me, and I haven't got a clue what to do. Then she hands me a lifeline.

'Where are you off to?' she asks, and suddenly the brain freeze is over. It all comes rushing in.

'Just school,' I tell her. That was all I needed. Just the right prompt. And now the thing that never fails me has kicked in, and I'm firing on all cylinders. 'We've got this careers class today,' I tell her. 'We have to do this fake interview role play, as if we're applying for a job.'

Mum nods. 'What's the job?' she asks.

I don't even stop to think. 'Management consultant in a corporate chain,' I say. I have no idea where these things come from. My brain must be like a scientific wonder or something.

'You're sure that's the job?' Mum replies. 'You're sure it's not junior warehouse assistant in a bottling hall?'

Crap. That sounds like it's probably what I was lined up for in my dad's place. I start wishing I'd read that form properly, so's I'd know for sure. All I can do is ride it out.

'No,' I say. 'It's not that. The teacher said this would make a more difficult interview.'

Mum doesn't look like she's about to laugh any more. 'Come off it, Jack,' she says, getting up off the telephone chair and heading towards the kitchen. 'I know exactly what's going on. And I've already phoned the factory and told them they'll be one applicant short for their interviews this morning.'

Busted!

Suddenly, I can't believe what I'm hearing. All I can think is I must still be upstairs in bed, and the big orange shape overtook me without me knowing about it. I'm certain this must be a dream. I come down to the bottom of the stairs and Mum turns to face me.

'What's the matter?' she says. 'Cat got your tongue?'

I think it must have. I think it must have got my brain as well. All I can do is stand and stare at her, then ask how she found out.

'Who . . . ?'

'Ray,' she says. 'He phoned first thing this morning and told me everything. He said he wanted to save you from ruining your talents. Whatever they might be.'

Then she wanders into the kitchen and starts clattering.

I'm speechless.

Uncle Ray! The big fat crazy bastard. I can't believe it. And all at once it hits me: I'm free. I'm free and it's not my fault. I'm off the hook, and Dad's got someone else to blame. I did everything I could. Uncle Ray's face looms up large in my imagination, with its black eye and its broken chin, and if I could I think I would probably kiss it.

'Get back up to your room and change,' Mum says. 'Get your school clothes on. It's over, Jack.'

I try my best to look hurt and disappointed, in case there's ever a point in the far distant future when she talks to Dad again. She might tell him about this moment, so I do everything I can to look crushed. Then I almost float back up the stairs.

While I'm eating breakfast, Mum tells me she'll be driving me to school, to make sure that's where I go. And to make sure I stay there. This is all good. It clears me of any responsibility for not turning up at the interview. Even if I wanted to trick my way there, it couldn't be done.

I wait till Mum goes out of the room for a minute, then knock up a text to Dad.

'We've been rumbled!' it says. 'Uncle Ray told Mum everything. She stayed at home and cancelled the interview.'

I send it out just as Mum comes back in, then I turn my phone off in case he texts back and Mum gets wind of what's going on.

'Hurry up,' she tells me. 'You're going to be late again.'

Then she stomps around the kitchen for a while, muttering things I can't really hear over the crunch of my cereal.

We don't talk much on the way to school. The muttering continues, but I manage to zone it out and start thinking about my dominoes again. Should I really go all the way back to the start, I wonder? Do I really need a new plan? I could ask Drew Thornton to come swimming, then steal all his clothes while he's getting changed, and have Elsie positioned somewhere suitable for that. Or I could put a wasp or a worm down the back of his shirt and hope he'll strip off in the playground trying to get rid of it. I can tell I'm just being silly now, but I'm in a silly mood. Being free of the interview has got me all full of the funny stuff, and I even consider just running into school and ripping Drew's clothes off in a fit of noonday madness. Elsie couldn't argue with that.

By the time we're getting close to school though, I start to sober up. The Coco Pops have stopped making my fingers tingle, and I'm thinking clearly again. I know my original plan is the way to go really. I've come too far with it to give up now, and the belief that I can talk Cyrus round comes back full force. I start to recognise the Uncle Ray Intervention for the good omen it is. It's a sign that my luck has changed, and I have to ride the wave of good fortune while it's carrying me along in the right direction. I have to let it help me talk Cyrus into doing what he's been refusing to do.

'I'll still be sitting here when it's time for your interview,' Mum says, as we pull up at the school gates. 'Don't bother trying to sneak out and go down there. I'll be waiting for you.'

'I didn't want to go in the first place,' I tell her, but she doesn't reply so I open the door and merge into the crowd outside.

'I'm disappointed in you, Jack,' she shouts as I follow the randoms down into the playground. I look around a bit, pretending I'm trying to work out who's being shouted at. A little leaf out of Chris Yates's book. On a smaller scale.

I've still got ten minutes left before it's time for registration, so I make my way round the back of the old building and head down towards the bins, looking for Cyrus. I'm in luck. He's there with the same crowd as yesterday, doing the same weird thing in the circle with the phones. Cyrus is all caught up in it, jerking about and making strange noises, so I take the opportunity to get as close to him as I can, then I just stand and wait. They all do that jerking thing for what seems like ages, then one of them shouts, 'Bam it!' and they stop for a minute and regroup.

I take my chance.

'Cyrus,' I say.

He turns round and looks at me, then he shakes his head.

'Get lost!' he says.

'I wanted to apologise for yesterday,' I tell him.

'Good for you. I don't want to know.'

He fiddles with his phone then lifts it back up to where the others are holding theirs. I move even closer to him and speak more quietly.

'I think I've thought up a way to get at Chris Yates,' I say.

'Risk free.'

He doesn't seem to respond at first, then he pulls his phone back a bit. I'm starting to get to him, but he's trying not to show it.

'Can we meet up at lunchtime to talk about it?' I ask, and he doesn't say no. He lifts his phone up close to his face and pretends he's doing something with it again. Then he speaks without turning round to look at me.

'Where?' he says.

'Somewhere quiet,' I say. 'Round behind the games hall?'

'When?' he asks.

'Half twelve? Something like that?'

'Be there,' he tells me, then he gets fully involved in the phone madness again. I walk away and leave them to it.

I certainly will be there.

19

During the morning break, after a mind-numbing double of Maths, I track down Chris Yates and tell him my cousin Harry is ready to stand in for him. Yatesy is on his own down near the Art classes, staring at a broken calculator that's lying in the grass, and drawing it in his notebook.

'When's it going to happen?' he asks, and I tell him I just need to square it with Cyrus first. Then I decide to chance my arm and see if I can fix a date for the Drew Thornton Session.

'How about this weekend?' I ask him. 'Can you do it on Saturday?'

'We'll see,' Yatesy says. 'Talk to me when your cousin's done his thing.'

'But you'll be in the clear by the weekend,' I tell him. 'I can guarantee it. Let's set it up now.'

He puts a few more lines in his notebook and then holds it out at arm's length. It's a pretty good drawing.

'Cyrus wants blood,' he says. 'You'll have trouble with him. All he cares about is seeing me expelled.'

I act surprised, as if I didn't know anything about it, and Yatesy nods.

'The bitch is angry,' he says.

He keeps scribbling away, rubbing things out and drawing them back in, and I decide to see if I can get any information that will help me get round Cyrus. Even just a kilobyte.

'What was the fight about anyway?' I ask. 'What started it?'

'Have you ever spoken to him?' Yatesy says.

I nod. 'Just once.'

'That's enough,' he says. 'If you've spoken to him once, you know what it was about.'

Fair point.

'Just that?' I say. 'Nothing else?'

Yatesy nods. 'Just that. And he kept going on about me being a bohemian. As if it was an insult or something. Did my head in.'

'What's a bohemian?' I say, and Yatesy screws his face up.

'You know,' he says. 'Like an artist. Somebody who doesn't buy into the bullshit. A freethinker.'

I decide he probably means somebody who paints his mum and dad naked without thinking it's weird, then I pretend I'd known what it meant all along, and I'd just forgotten.

'That,' I say. 'He thinks that's an insult?'

Yatesy nods.

'I'll find a way round him,' I say. 'Don't worry about it.'

'Good luck,' he says, and he draws some grass round about the calculator. Then he rubs it out again.

'So how about Saturday?' I ask.

'Maybe,' he says. 'I need to wait till your cousin's been to Bailey. That's just how it is, Jackdaw.'

I can see I'm not going to get any further. I know when I'm wasting my time. I stand watching him drawing for a bit longer, then I wander off and leave him to it.

* * *

After that, it's Sergeant Monahan for the rest of the morning. There's a bright spot when he calls Wendy Gillis out to the front of the class to elevate the book, and she refuses to do it.

'My brother says there's a European directive against it,' she tells him. 'You can't make us do that any more.'

The top of Monahan's ears go red, and he stands pressing his hands down on his desk. He caught Wendy watching a clip of a moron eating a spider on her phone, when we were supposed to be listening to his analogue upload about the first plane to drop a bomb or something, and he's not happy.

'Perhaps we should go and ask the headmaster if your brother's right then,' the Sergeant says. 'He's bound to know all about it.'

He walks over to the door and opens it, holding it for Wendy to go first. She stands without moving by the side of her desk, where she's been since the Sergeant shouted, 'On your feet!' at the start of the proceedings.

'Shall we?' the Sergeant asks. 'I'm sure the rest of the class are keen to know if Mr Bailey would agree with your brother too.'

Wendy still doesn't move and the Sergeant lets the door fall shut. He goes to his shelf and brings down the weighty volume, then he puts it on his desk. Wendy looks at one of her mad friends for a while, then at another one. They both pretend they don't really know her, and she sighs and stomps out to the front of the class, where she picks the book up and gets started on the usual business with it.

The rest of the lesson is a giga-snore. Monahan continues to Bluetooth his nonsense about bombs and planes and general destruction, and the lack of sleep from the night before starts to catch up with me. A couple of times I see the big orange shape and hear the dream voices, and I have to take serious measures to make sure I don't pass out. I sneak my phone from my pocket and switch it on underneath the desk, to see if anything has come in from my dad. Being caught using my phone would probably get me a longer stint with the book than falling asleep in class, but I have more control over whether Monahan catches me with the phone or not, and I know the sense of danger will keep me awake. I watch Monahan now as if I'm listening to every word he says, and just glance at the phone when I'm absolutely sure his attention is engaged elsewhere.

The phone vibrates almost immediately, but it's a good five minutes before I get the chance to look at what's come in. When I do, I'm pleased to see my dad's taking the whole situation relatively calmly.

'That arse-biscuit!' his text says. 'I'll kill him. If your mum doesn't kill me first.'

I do all I can not to laugh, and then I go back to staring at the Sergeant.

A few minutes later, the phone vibrates again and a new text comes in. This time it's almost fifteen minutes before I can even glance at it. Monahan appears to have picked me out as his star pupil for this lesson, probably because I'm the only person who's actually looking at him, and he starts delivering most of his pitch exclusively to me. It's only when Grant Fraser's earphone jack slips out of the socket on his phone, and the tiny speaker starts blasting out the crappy music he's been listening to, that Monahan finally turns his attention to other matters and I'm free to read my dad's latest missive.

'I need one of your schemes, pal,' it says. 'Help me out here. What can I do to fix things with your mum?'

Luckily, the Sergeant is going all out on this Grant Fraser thing, and I even have time to reply. Wendy gets sent back to her seat, still muttering about the European Parliament, and Grant steps into the spotlight.

'I'll see what I can do,' I write, then I send it and turn the phone off. I don't have the heart to tell him that even my formidable talents can't help him out of this one. What could he possibly say to fix it with Mum?

'I slipped on a patch of spilt whiskey and fell into arranging the interview'?

Or, 'I pressed the wrong button when I was trying to set up a meeting for him at university'?

He's dug his own grave this time. Plus, all my RAM is given over to working on what I'm going to say to Cyrus. I don't have anything left to spare.

By the time the Sergeant resumes business again, I'm wide awake. With the phone switched off, I don't need to be looking at him any more, and I soon manage to zone out his stream of data about spitfires and doodlebugs and mushroom clouds, and get down to thinking about what really matters: letting that wave of good luck carry me on to a victory with Cyrus.

20

When I arrive at the games hall Cyrus is already waiting for me, just him on his own. He's eating something soggy out of a paper bag, and he holds it up to me as I approach.

I peer inside the bag. It looks awful.

'What's that?' I ask him.

'Macaroni and cheese,' he says. 'Made it in Hospitality.'

He asks me if I want any but I tell him I'm not hungry, even though I'm really starving.

'Why's it in a bag?' I ask him.

'Forgot my Tupperware,' he says. 'Benson wouldn't lend me a tub. Silly old cow.'

We sit down on the grass, over by the fence, and he pushes another handful of the yellow stuff into his face. It smells terrible. I didn't know it was possible to feel sick and starving at the same time, until now.

'So how do we get Yatesy?' Cyrus says. Straight in. 'This better be good. I'm missing Boodle for this.'

'What's Boodle?' I ask him, and instantly wish I hadn't. It turns out Boodle is the retard phone game he's always playing, and he launches into a long description of all its pathetic rules and a list of his scores. Then, just when I think I'm about to pass out, he tells me I'm wasting too much of his time, and that he's only here to talk about my plan.

'So what is it?' he says. 'What are you going to do?'

'I'm going to make you tell Bailey you fought Harry, rather than Yatesy,' I think to myself. 'I'm not sure how I'm going to do it yet, but it'll happen.'

I just need the right bit of information.

'Here's what worries me,' I tell him then. 'I'm scared the plan I've got at the moment might let Yatesy off too lightly. I have to make sure I get him as badly as he got you.'

And I ask him exactly what Yatesy did to him.

'He ruined my life,' Cyrus says. 'Totally.'

It's not exactly the windfall I'm looking for.

'I thought you just got a three-day suspension,' I say, and he nods.

'I did,' he says, 'but that was only the start of it.'

And he begins unleashing the good stuff. It turns out his parents have really gone to town on him. He's been grounded since then until the exams are over, and he's not allowed to do anything he wants to do, even at home. His dad drops him off at the gate in the morning, and picks him up again as soon as the bell rings for the end of the day. They've even banned him from going online except for homework, and his dad locked the Xbox away in the garage.

'I want Yatesy to pay for all of that,' Cyrus says. 'And . . . some other stuff. Plus, he's a bohemian.'

'I hate bohemians,' I assure him. 'They freak me out.'

'They're disgusting,' Cyrus says. 'They undermine the whole fabric of society.'

I decide I should have looked into this whole bohemian thing a bit more. I'm starting to get out of my depth, so I turn the conversation back to the matter in hand.

'I've got a new idea forming,' I tell Cyrus, and he looks at me eagerly. 'What was that you said about some other things though? What things were they?'

He pokes about in his bag for a minute. 'It doesn't matter,' he says. The bag is starting to tear down near the bottom, where it's all wet. Bits of it are staying stuck to the food now too, but he doesn't seem to notice.

'I have to know the whole story,' I tell him. 'We have to get Yatesy for everything. We can't let him get anything over on you.'

Cyrus sighs. He tears the top part of the bag away, and he's left with just a horrible mushy mess of paper and yellow gunk in his hands. He keeps on eating it though.

'My parents won't let me go to the school dance,' he says quietly, and keeps his eyes on the gunk.

'You want to go to that?' I ask him. 'Really?'

He nods, still looking down. 'I'm meant to go with Amy Gilchrist,' he says. 'She said she'd go with me weeks ago. But now she's going with Yinka instead, if I can't make it.'

I almost just blurt out what I'm thinking. 'Amy Gilchrist? Really? You want to go to the school dance with her?' Amy Gilchrist only comes second on the weirdo scale to Elsie Green. She has this strange kind of smile, and she's always making this weird noise in class when everything's quiet. It just seems to come out on its own. But then I remember Cyrus is pretty much in that same category of weird himself, and I stop myself saying any of it just in time.

'That's harsh,' I say instead, and the wheels start to turn. 'How long have you been after Amy for?'

'Forever,' Cyrus says. 'I wish I could kill Yatesy. I really do.'

Something is starting to happen. My fingers are tingling, and my synapses are firing. All my binary data is starting to flow. I sit quietly for a minute and let it happen, trying not to watch Cyrus licking the last of the gunk off his fingers, then rubbing his hands on the grass, then licking his fingers again.

I feel as if I'm probably doing Amy Gilchrist a disservice by trying to get her together with Cyrus, but I put that to one side and go out on a limb.

'We need to get you to that dance,' I say. 'Getting Yatesy back is important, but no matter how badly we hurt him you'll still have lost Amy. Nothing we can do to him will change that. You've got to get to that dance, Cyrus.'

He nods sadly. 'It can't be done though,' he says. 'You don't know my parents. It could never happen in a million years.'

'What if I told you I could make it happen?' I say. 'This is what I do, Cyrus. I'm an ideas man. I think I can get you there.'

He looks at me with a kind of disbelief in his eyes. 'If you could do that,' he says, 'if you could, Jack . . .'

'Call me Jackdaw,' I tell him, and he nods.

'Jackdaw . . .' he says, and I trust to the wave of good fortune that's carrying me along, and I strike while the iron's hot.

'Remember my cousin Harry?' I say, and Cyrus nods. 'He wants to go to university, but his dad won't let him. His dad's kind of a bohemian, and he wants Harry to be a bohemian too. But Harry wants to be just like . . . society. That's why I'm trying to help him.'

'I hate parents,' Cyrus says. 'All of them.'

'How about this then,' I say. 'I'll come up with a plan that really sticks it to Yatesy good and proper, and another one to make sure you get to the school dance. I can do that. No problem. But you'll have to do something for me in return.'

'Anything,' Cyrus says, which is exactly what I was hoping for.

'Help Harry out,' I say. 'Let him go to Bailey and take the rap for being in that fight with you. Say he was the guy if Bailey asks you anything about it. That's all. That's all I'm asking.'

It's quite clear that when he said 'anything', this wasn't in the list of things he was thinking about. He probably thought I was after his Xbox or something. But he thinks it over. He sits looking towards the games hall, and he stays like that for a while.

'But then Yatesy doesn't get punished for the fight,' he says at last. 'How can that be right, Jackdaw?'

'I admit it's not ideal,' I tell him. 'But you have to remember we'll hit him with something bigger, later on. Think of how smug he'll feel thinking he's off the hook, then think of the shock he'll get when we hit him with the real thing.'

Cyrus continues to sit silently, then he slowly begins to nod. He gets up into a crouch, and starts rubbing his hands. Then he stands right up.

'That could work,' he says. 'What kind of thing would you do?'

'Nothing at all,' I think to myself. 'As soon as you've done the business with Bailey that's the end of the matter.' The thing is, Chris Yates seems okay to me, and Cyrus is so unpleasant, with his bizarre dislike of bohemians for no apparent reason, that it'll be a bonus to get one up on him.

'Something big,' I say. 'Something that'll ruin his life. I'll probably do something to make him fail his Art exam, so he can't go to art school. If he got expelled for this fight, he could probably still get in somewhere else and do his Art exam there. But if I make sure he can't pass it, no matter how many times he tries, that'll be worth its weight in gold.'

'You're an evil genius,' Cyrus says, and he smiles.

'So I'll tell Harry he can go to Bailey?' I say, and Cyrus nods enthusiastically.

'Totally,' he says. 'I'll even go with him. And I'll erase that recording off my phone too. Just as soon as I'm back on for going to the dance.'

'How about letting Harry go to Bailey this afternoon?' I say. 'And how about erasing that message right now?'

'Not a chance,' Cyrus says, and I can tell this is as far as the wave is going to carry me, for today. I have another couple of shots at him, but it leads nowhere. So in the end I give it up and reach out to shake his hand, forgetting all about the gunk and the licking until it's too late. We shake hands in that old-fashioned way, just to seal the deal, then I hurry off to the toilets and scrub and scrub all the way up to the elbow, to avoid contracting some kind of weird macaroni disease.

So I'm almost there. All my dominoes are back in place. Chris Yates will get his pardon, Harry will get to go to university, and Elsie Green will have her perverted desires for Drew Thornton fulfilled. All I have to do is make sure Cyrus gets to that stupid school dance. That's all.

How the hell am I going to manage that?

21

When I get home from school, after another hard afternoon at the coalface of boredom, I see the sign which means the Regular Madness will move up a few notches to the Special Occasion Madness later tonight: a packed suitcase sitting in the hallway. I didn't manage to come up with anything for my dad. There was a point in Geography when I thought something was stirring, something about him owning up to Mum that he'd been in a brawl with Uncle Ray the other night, and then telling her it was only a work experience place I'd been coming in to see about. But it didn't really form into anything solid. My circuits were still a bit overheated from my session with Cyrus, and I think part of my operating system had already gone to work on coming up with something to get Cyrus to the school dance. So, in the end, I just sent Dad a text that said I was still thinking, and that I hadn't come up with anything yet. And that's how things stayed.

I notice the suitcase just as Mum comes out of the kitchen with her face all angry looking, probably because she thinks it's my dad that's just come through the door. When she sees it's me she looks kind of disappointed, but more friendly at the same time too.

'Didn't you go to work?' I ask her, and she tells me she didn't.

'I had a few things to catch up on here,' she says. 'I just worked at home this afternoon.'

Perhaps you're thinking the packed suitcase lying at the bottom of the stairs is hers. It isn't. You might even be thinking it's my dad's; that Mum's thrown a few of his essentials in there, and she'll hand it to him as soon as he walks through the door, and tell him to get out. But that's not how it works during the Special Occasion Madness. The suitcase is mine, and it's me who'll be getting the elbow pretty soon.

'Uncle Ray's coming round in about twenty minutes,' Mum tells me. 'You'll be staying with him for the next couple of nights, just while your dad and I work things out. It'll be easier for you there.'

I'm surprised she still thinks she even needs to explain this stuff to me any more.

'Can't I go somewhere else, though?' I ask her. 'It's insane at Uncle Ray's. He's a crazy man.'

'The only other place is Grandpa's,' she says, but I know that isn't really an option. I tried that once before, and it ended up with Mum and Dad having to come and collect me from the police station. Everything went okay for the first couple of days, then on the third morning I was crashing about in the kitchen trying to work out how to use Grandpa's ancient hardware, when he threw the kitchen door open, still wearing his pyjamas, and picked up a big bread knife that was lying on the table.

'All right, sonny boy!' he shouted at me. 'Get yourself into the living room.'

I thought it was a joke to begin with, and I started laughing, but he didn't like that.

'Find this funny, do you?' he said. 'I'll show you funny if you don't get moving. I've dealt with your kind before. Come on, get in there.'

I got quite scared then, and just did as he told me. When we were in the living room he kept the knife pointing at me, and picked up the phone to call the police.

'It's me, Grandpa,' I kept saying to him. 'Jack. The Jackdaw.'

But he kept telling me he knew all about my sort, and that this was a victory for the little man, and within five minutes the police arrived and drove me to the station, thinking I was a burglar. Then Mum and Dad had to come down to confirm I was who I said I was, and to take me home.

'Okay,' I say to Mum. 'You win. Uncle Ray's it is.'

My big fat crazy uncle is as good as his word. Within twenty minutes he turns up in his bampot taxi, and starts hammering his horn out on the street. Mum hands me my suitcase and tells me not to worry about anything.

'It's only for a night or two,' she says. 'Just until we work out if your dad and I have any kind of future together. Then you can come back.'

This is the routine I have to go through every time. The reality of it is, in two or three days, even the Regular Madness will be gone for a while. Mum and Dad will be like two new best friends, seeing who can be the nicest to each other, and indulging in a bit too much parent kissing in front of me for my liking. There'll be a few things missing from the house, a chair and a couple of plants maybe, or a few ornaments and one of the small tables. Then I'll find it all lying by the bin when I take the rubbish out at some point. There might be a couple of new cracks or dents in the woodwork around one of the doors, or a new mark or two on the walls or the floor when I get back, but that'll be the full extent of the damage. Mum knows this as well as I do, but I think she must enjoy the drama of it all or something.

'Take care,' she says quietly, and I bump my suitcase over the threshold and drag it down the path, towards the waiting madman.

'Don't worry about a thing, Mary,' he shouts, getting out of the car. 'I'll make sure he's as right as rain.'

Then he hurls my suitcase onto the back seat, ruffles up my hair, and we're off, with me clinging onto the dashboard for dear life and him making that god awful noise he calls 'singing opera'.

22

There are three main things an ideas man needs when he's working on The Big One: the first two are peace and quiet, and the third is plenty of privacy to do his thinking in. I know from past experience I won't be getting very much of any of them at Uncle Ray's place. Uncle Ray will put paid to the first two, with his constant jabbering and his crashing about in the kitchen, his insistence on always having at least two TVs and one radio on at any particular time, and then the 'opera singing' on top of all that. Harry, on the other hand, should take care of the privacy issue. Whenever I get dumped at Uncle Ray's house I always have to share Harry's room, and sleep on his floor on a blow-up mattress which constantly leaks. The worst thing is, when Harry's not at school, he never *ever* leaves his room. He's always playing chess against himself, getting stuck into his school books, messing about on his computer, or sticking bits onto model cars with a brain-warping glue. You can't even get any time to yourself in the bathroom. If you ever try to spend more than thirty-five seconds in there, Uncle Ray comes and starts banging on the door, shouting about needing to 'quickly fill in a few clues on the crossword' or to 'batter on some aftershave for the bowling club'.

It's a far from ideal situation, especially under the current circumstances.

When the hair-raising taxi ride draws to a close, I spend about ten minutes in the kitchen with Uncle Ray, pretending to drink the beer he gives me in celebration of my interview being cancelled, and listening to him hammering on about a variety of crazy men he's had in his taxi over the past few days. Then he tells me to take my suitcase upstairs and get 'settled in', while he knocks up some dinner for us. 'Gourmet fare', he calls it. I thank him again for saving me from a life of label licking, and then drag my things up to Harry's bedroom and bang on the door. Harry doesn't answer.

'I thought I told you I didn't want to see you again,' he says, when I open the door and go in anyway. 'If you've brought my suit back just throw it on the bed and get lost.'

'I haven't brought your suit back,' I tell him.

'Even better,' he says. 'That means you can just go.'

I heave my suitcase up onto his bed and sit down beside it. 'I can't go anywhere,' I tell him quietly. 'I've moved in. We're room-mates again.'

And like you can probably imagine, he's not particularly thrilled by this breaking news. He picks up his chess pieces, one at a time, and starts throwing them at the wall.

'No way,' he shouts. 'Not again. You can sleep out in the hall this time.'

'It's nothing to do with me,' I tell him. 'Blame your dad. It's all his fault.'

'How?'

'He told my mum about that interview, and now she and my dad are locked into the Special Occasion Madness. So I have to stay here till it's over.'

'I hate my dad,' Harry says. 'I absolutely hate him.'

I open my suitcase and start putting some of my things out on a chair. I might as well make myself at home, I decide, and I don't want my clothes to get too many creases in them.

'It's not all bad news though,' I say to Harry after a while, when his constant muttering to himself is starting to ease off, and his rate of throwing the chess pieces is down to about one a minute. 'I've brought some of the good stuff too.'

He doesn't answer.

'We're back on for the whole Chris Yates thing,' I say, and I can tell he doesn't believe me. 'I spoke to Cyrus again today. It's all arranged. He says he'll okay your story with Bailey.'

'Bullshit,' Harry says, but I nod. 'I don't believe you,' he says.

'Why would I make it up?'

'So you don't have to sleep in the hall.'

'I'll sleep in the hall if you want,' I tell him. 'It doesn't make any difference to me.'

That gets him. All the red colour starts to disappear from his face, and he stands up and looks at me.

'Genuinely?' he says. 'Cyrus really said that?'

'Totally.'

'Jesus!' Harry says, and he starts picking up all of his scattered chess pieces and putting them back in place on the squares of the board. 'This is unbelievable, Jack.'

Meanwhile, I'm unpacking my bathroom stuff and wondering

why Mum's put a pouch full of golf balls in my suitcase. Why would she do that?

'This is incredible,' Harry says. 'How did you manage to talk Cyrus round?'

'Easily,' I say. 'I told him I'd do him a favour.'

'What favour?'

I take out a couple of the golf balls and look at them for a minute, then I hold them up for Harry to see.

'What the hell are these?' I ask.

'Golf balls,' he says distractedly.

'I know that, but why have I got them? Why did my mum put them in my case?'

He shrugs.

I hunt around in the pouch to see if there's anything else in there, but there's nothing. Just the golf balls. I think my mum must be finally losing her mind.

'What favour did you say you'd do for Cyrus?' Harry asks again, and I zip up the pouch and throw it back into my suitcase.

'I told him I'd get him to the school dance,' I say. 'His parents banned him from going, because of the fight. So I told him I'll get him there.'

Harry slumps down in his seat, and some of the red colour comes back into his face again. 'Crap,' he says. 'We're screwed. That'll never happen.'

'Of course it will,' I say. 'This is my forte, Harry. It's what I do. Don't worry about any of that.'

'Do you even know who Cyrus's parents are?' Harry asks. 'He's got like the strictest parents in the whole school. You'll never sort this one out.'

That isn't the kind of news I want to hear, but I push my empty suitcase under the bed and brave it out.

'Of course I will,' I say. 'It's already sorted. Just about. I've got the perfect plan bubbling away. I just need to work on some of the finer details. You're going to university. I can guarantee it.'

He starts to rise up out of the slump a little bit. The red colour begins to disappear again.

'You've got a plan already?' he says. 'Honestly?'

'I'll give you it in writing if you want,' I say. 'It's all systems go.'

'And then I can definitely go to Bailey? No more strings attached?'

'That's what I'm telling you,' I say, and he's up on his feet again.

'Do you need any help?' he says. 'Is there anything I can do to help with the plan? Do you need a wingman?'

A wingman!

'I don't think so,' I tell him, trying not to laugh. 'I'll let you know if I do, but I think the whole thing's self-functioning.'

'Is there anything else I can do to help? Anything at all?'

'Just give me some space to think when I need it,' I say. 'That's all. Can you do that?'

'Absolutely,' he says, and he starts moving his alarm clock and his pyjamas and stuff. 'You can have the bed too,' he tells me. 'You need to be in tip-top condition for this. I'll sleep on the floor.'

'Straight up?'

'Straight up,' he says, and he drags the plastic mattress out and starts pumping it up there and then. I watch him struggling with it for a while, and then I lie down on his bed, staring up at the ceiling and listening to Uncle Ray breaking something or other downstairs.

Result!

23

As I'm sitting in French the next morning though, looking out the window at a train that hasn't moved in almost half an hour, I start to wonder if there's really much advantage to having the bed in Harry's room. Uncle Ray's noise goes on so late into the night, and starts up again so early in the morning, that it's practically impossible to sleep there anyway. I spent most of the night sitting up at Harry's desk, watching the TV with a pair of headphones on, while he snored behind me on the blow-up. I was like a zombie by the time Uncle Ray drove us to school in his taxi, still hammering the opera.

I struggle all morning just trying to keep it together. There's a point where the train I'm staring at just disappears, and I can't work out what's happened. One moment I'm staring at it and it's there, the next moment I'm still staring at it but it's totally gone. It didn't drive away or anything, just vanished. Then I realise I must have fallen asleep for a few minutes without knowing about it, and it freaks me out a little bit. Luckily no one else seems to have noticed. Luckily I couldn't have been snoring, or talking in my sleep.

I do manage to get it together enough to interface with

Cyrus at lunchtime again though. I find him sitting over by the window in the dining hall, where he'd been a couple of days ago during the Elsie Green debacle, and I set about getting the full details of his grounding and of his set-up at home, just so's I know exactly what I'm up against. I've got my English jotter out, and I make a bunch of notes in it while I'm talking to him, which isn't something I usually have to do. Everything I need to know usually stays right there in my head, but my head's in such a mess from all the lack of sleep and everything that I don't trust it to keep hold of anything, so I write it all down.

It turns out the thing Harry was trying to tell me about Cyrus's parents is that they're pacifists. I don't really know what that means at first, but Cyrus explains that his parents are completely against any kind of fighting. Or violence. When he was a kid, he wasn't allowed to have any toy guns or soldiers or tanks or anything like that, and that's why this thing with Chris Yates has landed him in it so deeply. I wish I'd known about this pacifist thing the other day, in History. Maybe I could've used it against Monahan, told him I was one of those, and got myself excused from all that war boredom he was peddling.

'So it's like you've gone against your mum and dad's religion?' I ask Cyrus.

'It's not a religion, dumb-ass,' he tells me.

But I write that down in my notebook anyway.

I also put this bit in about when his parents were becoming pacifists in the first place. Cyrus was still quite young, and his dad bought him a bow and arrow, and then when his mum found out she went ape-shit and took it off him. My brain is still working just enough for me to recognise this means

Cyrus's mum is probably more of a pacifist than his dad is, even though they're both totally strict on it now. It's possible there might be some way to use this to my advantage. Apart from that, my jotter is just filled up with all the details of the mess Cyrus is in, and of his set-up at home. Ever since he came back to school, after his suspension, his dad drives him in in the morning, and picks him up at the gates at the end of the day. He's not allowed any kind of social life at all, and he has to have these sessions in the evenings with his parents, where they contemplate peace and talk about the effects of violence in the world each day. At the weekends he has to go with them wherever they're going, and all the rest of the time he has to study. His ban isn't going to be lifted until he gets his exam results.

'What about their jobs?' I ask him. 'Where do your mum and dad work?'

'My dad works at home,' he says. 'My mum works in the primary school.'

'Do they ever go out together in the evenings and leave you on your own?' I ask, and he shakes his head. 'What about leaving you with somebody else?'

'Sometimes my grandma comes round and they go out somewhere. Not much.'

I write that down anyway. I might see something in it when my head starts to work again.

'So what about the school dance?' I ask him. 'Why are they so against you going? Is that 'cause they're pacifists too?'

'Are you mad?' he says. 'Why would pacifists be against a dance?'

'I don't know,' I tell him. 'I don't know anything about it. It's your religion.'

'It's not a religion!' he screeches. 'It's just a thing. I've already told you that. They just won't let me go because they know I want to go. As a punishment. Are you sure you can do anything about this? You don't seem to know anything about anything.'

'It's all under control,' I tell him. 'I just didn't get much sleep last night. I'll be all right again tomorrow. Don't worry about it. You'll be at the dance.'

I have to admit, though, that as the afternoon wears on I begin to wonder how I'm ever going to pull it off. I try to read through my notes in Science, but all the words just sort of swim in front of my eyes and I can't even make out what any of them are. And things at Uncle Ray's place don't get any better. The chaos continues unabated, and Harry's idea of giving me plenty of space seems to revolve around him sitting staring at me wherever I am, saying, 'Anything yet, Jackdaw?' every five or ten minutes. The only thing I seem to be on course for at the moment is a full psychotic episode.

Get this though: Elsie Green finally accepted my friend request. I'd forgotten all about it, but I was using Harry's computer to carry on the argument I've been having with Sandy Hammil, about whether it was him who told everyone Elsie kissed me or not, when the little red dot suddenly appeared up in the corner of my profile. I couldn't even guess who it was from, my head was so mashed. But the worst of it was, when I clicked it open, I noticed she'd sent me a message too.

'I don't want this to give you the wrong idea,' it said. 'This doesn't mean your suit has found favour with me. But I don't want to add to your torture. I know what the heart of the lover will do. Be strong, Jack. Elsie.'

Jesus Christ!

It got me so wound up I even started typing a reply to her, telling her what I really thought of her in an attempt to make her see this madness was all in her head. But I realised the last thing I need is to have her refuse to help with my programming, after everything. So I used my anger instead to type up a reply to Sandy, telling him he must be drunk if he thought I'd believe everybody had just seen Elsie kissing me. It was quite a sizzler. Then I went downstairs to face the 'Something Special' Uncle Ray had promised to make us for dinner.

'So how's the latest scheme going?' Uncle Ray says, as I sit down and try to work out what exactly the Something Special is. 'Regale us with tales of your latest exploits, Mr Jackdaw.'

In my delirium, I have the mad idea Uncle Ray might be able to come up with a solution that will help me if I tell him about it, so I decide to lay it out for him.

'I'm helping one of my friends,' I say. 'His parents have banned him from going to the school dance, and there's a girl he'll lose if he can't take her to it. So I'm working on a way to get him there.'

Uncle Ray slaps his knee and starts creasing up.

'I love it,' he says. 'You're a regular Figaro, Jackie D.'

Then he points his fork at Harry. 'You could learn a thing or two from this boy,' he says. 'That's the way to go about life, Harry. Get right in about it. Mix things up a bit.'

He shuffles some of the stuff from his plate into his mouth, and thinks for a minute. God knows how he manages to think with all the noise that's going on. There's a TV and a radio both playing in the kitchen, and then there's the noise from the TV that's blaring away in the living room too. But after a bit, Uncle Ray starts nodding, then he swallows some beer to push down all the food that's in his mouth.

'Here's how you go about that, Jack,' he says, tapping his fork on his plate. 'All you need are some pillows. Your pal tells his parents he's not feeling well on the night of the dance, and he goes up to bed early. He fills the bed with the pillows, so's it looks as if he's in there. Then you're underneath his bedroom window, holding onto the bottom of a rope ladder to keep it steady. He climbs down and whammo! You whisk him off to the dance and if his parents come up to check on him they see the pillows in the bed and think he's sleeping soundly. After the dance he climbs back up the rope ladder, and no one's any the wiser. How does that sound?'

'Pretty crappy,' I say. 'Unless we're living in a lame children's comic.' Or else I say, 'Pretty good, Uncle Ray. I'll give that some thought and see if I can use it.' I'm so confused by all the noise, and so exhausted and ready to fall asleep that I'm not even sure what I say. I meant to think the first one and say the second, but maybe I did it the other way around. I'm too bewildered to even know.

'You're a spunky one,' Uncle Ray laughs. 'I want you to watch this boy while he's here, Harry. Get versed in some of his ways. Let some of his spunk rub off on you.'

Harry looks appalled. 'Dad!' he says. 'That doesn't mean what you think it means.'

'Don't tell me what I think I mean,' Uncle Ray shouts, banging his beer bottle down on the table. 'I'll show you exactly what I'm talking about, son. Tell him, Jack. Tell him what your favourite subject in school is.'

'French,' I say, trying to give Harry a sympathetic look.

'Exactly,' Uncle Ray shouts. 'Now tell him why.'

'Because the French class has got the best view of the trains.'

Uncle Ray gets a major crease on. He starts slapping the table. 'You see, Harry,' he says, 'you see? That's what I'm talking about. Spunk! Now tell him what your second favourite subject is, Jack.'

'Arithmetic,' I say.

'For why?' Uncle Ray asks theatrically.

'Because it's got the best view of the river.'

Uncle Ray has heard all this a hundred times before. Mainly because he's asked me it ninety-nine times now, after I told him about it the first time. But he still laughs as if it's a brand-new joke with a brand-new punch line, and he points his fork at Harry while he's laughing. Harry just stares at him, screwing up his mouth.

'Have I told you what this one's been getting up to recently?' Uncle Ray says to me. 'Did you hear what I found him doing the other night when I walked into his room?'

'Shut up, Dad!' Harry says, and Uncle Ray's black eye starts to bulge and throb.

'Don't you dare tell me to shut up!' he shouts. 'Maybe when you've got a bit of your cousin's *zest* you can try something like that, but not while you're still choosing to behave like a titmouse. No way.'

And then it all kicks off properly. Uncle Ray gets going on a mad purple rant about the kind of food Harry wants to learn to make at university or something, while Harry just sits there staring at the table.

'Choux pastry!' Uncle Ray shouts. 'What in the name of

God is wrong with you, son? You've been watching too many of those morons on the telly. Prima donnas. Is my food not good enough for you or something?'

I look down at my plate and try to drown everything out by making an attempt at guessing what we're actually having for dinner. I'm pretty certain it's not a thing, but that's all I can work out about it. At least with pizza and peas you know there's pizza involved, and you know there are peas. You know it's not a thing, but you know what it's made up of. With Uncle Ray's Something Special, I can't even get that far.

It tastes all right though.

The whole titmouse thing carries on for quite a while, until I don't have very much of the Something Special left on my plate. The noise is insane. The televisions, the radio, the shouting and the banging of cups and cutlery. But in amongst it all I still manage to make out another noise, a noise that wasn't there before. And after a minute I recognise it's my phone. I pull it out of my pocket and see it's my mum calling. I hold it up to Uncle Ray and tell him I have to go and talk to her. He doesn't stop shouting at Harry, but he nods while he's doing it, and I get up from the table and clear out of there. Then I head for the front door, and go and stand outside, just to give myself half a chance of hearing whatever she's got to say.

24

I answer my phone full of hope that the Special Occasion Madness will be over, and I can just go home now. I know, in reality, that's not going to happen; the Special Occasion Madness is never over after one night. But the thought of my own quiet room where I can only hear one TV blaring downstairs, and where I can sleep in my kid bed for a whole glorious eight hours, makes me wish for it like crazy. And I tell myself there's a first time for everything.

'How are things?' Mum asks as soon as I push the button. She doesn't even say hello, or let me say hello, or anything like that.

'Pretty bad,' I tell her.

'How's Uncle Ray treating you? Is he feeding you properly?'

'I don't know,' I say. 'I think so.'

'What did you have for dinner tonight?'

'Something orange,' I say, 'with green bits in it. I'm not sure what it was.'

'For goodness' sake, Jack,' she replies. 'Surely you know what you had for dinner. Was it out of a packet or did Uncle Ray make it himself?'

'I don't know,' I tell her, 'I was upstairs with Harry. I think he made it himself.'

‘Did the orange colour look natural? Or was it artificial colouring? Tell your uncle Ray I don’t want you eating any E-numbers.’

‘Okay,’ I say. ‘Is it time to come home yet?’

‘Not yet,’ Mum says. ‘Dad and I are still talking. Is that traffic I can hear? Where are you?’

I watch my hopes from earlier crumble to dust, then I tell her that I’m just on the street outside the house.

‘What are you out there for?’ she says. ‘It’s cold tonight.’

‘It’s too noisy in the house to hear anything,’ I explain. ‘Uncle Ray’s shouting at Harry about being a titmouse.’

‘I hope he doesn’t shout at you,’ she says. ‘Does he? I won’t stand for him shouting at you.’

I tell her he doesn’t. ‘He likes me,’ I say. ‘He thinks I’m spunky. He says I’ve got zest.’

Mum laughs. ‘I suppose you are pretty spunky,’ she says. ‘Tell me about that orange colour again. Did it look artificial to you? Was it a foody orange, or did it look like it had been added in chemically?’

‘It was just orange,’ I tell her, ‘with green bits. I think I’d be okay at home while you and Dad are talking, Mum. It can’t be as loud as it is here. I can’t sleep. I think I’m getting hypertension again.’

‘It’s only for a couple of nights,’ Mum says. ‘You’ll get through it. A couple of nights without sleep won’t hurt you at your age. But tell Uncle Ray I don’t want you eating any E-numbers. If he’s giving you additives you’ll get out of balance. That’s probably where your hypertension is coming from.’

Then I get an idea.

'I've got this essay I have to put in in a couple of days' time,' I tell her. Put in? Is that what you do with an essay? It's not something I have much experience of, but I carry on with the thing anyway. 'It counts for the exam I think. And I can't get any work done on it. There's so much noise I can't even think about what I'm going to write.'

'Surely you can go to the school library,' she says.

'What for?'

'Well surely it's quiet in there. Isn't it?'

I don't think I know the answer to that question. I don't know if I've ever been in the school library. I vaguely remember a tour at the start of first year, when this teacher showed us round the whole school. We probably visited the library that day, but who knows if it was quiet or not?

'Should it be quiet?' I ask, and Mum laughs a little bit.

'Uncle Ray's right,' she says. 'You *are* zesty. Just work on your essay in the library, Jack. That's what it's there for. And remember to tell Uncle Ray about the additives, okay? What will you say to him?'

'No E-numbers.'

'Good. What about that green colour? Did that look natural? Was it just peppers or something?'

'I think Harry's shouting on me now, Mum,' I say. 'I better go. I'll tell Uncle Ray about the additives. Do you think I'll be able to come home tomorrow night?'

'Maybe,' Mum says. 'I'm sure it won't be too long. I'll phone you again tomorrow, either way. And good luck with the essay.'

'Thanks,' I say, and then I end the call. I can still hear some TVs from inside the house, but I can't hear Uncle Ray shouting at Harry anymore. I stay outside for a while anyway, though, considering this thing about the library. Is it quiet there? Maybe that was only in the olden days, when Mum was at school. But if it's true, maybe I could get some thinking done in there. Maybe I could do a clean-up operation on my brain and see if there's anything moving about. I decide to look into it first thing in the morning, and head back into the madhouse feeling a little bit better.

I was right about the shouting. Uncle Ray is sitting in the kitchen on his own when I get back inside, and Harry has gone up to his room to sulk. That's how Uncle Ray tells it anyway. He gives me this strange dessert that's quite hard, and tastes a bit like beer. He says he calls it The Stun Ray. It doesn't taste all that bad.

'How're things at home?' he asks, while I try to break bits off it with a spoon. 'Are they sorting it out?'

'I think so,' I tell him. 'I still can't go home yet.'

'No problem,' he says. 'I like having you here.'

I don't say anything to him about the E-numbers.

When I go upstairs, Harry doesn't talk to me for quite a while. He sits at his chessboard moving pieces about half-heartedly, and his face looks all grim and depressed. I think he's quite embarrassed that I saw Uncle Ray shouting at him like that, and I start to feel quite sorry for him. I can't wait to pull off this trick for Cyrus, so's life will get a bit better for Harry, and he won't get shouted at so much any more. Eventually he starts muttering about how much he hates his dad, and I tell him it's a pity he can't swap homes with Cyrus.

'I found out what the deal with his parents is,' I say. 'They're something called pacifists. The thing they hate most in the world is fighting. They'd like you a lot, Harry. And your dad would probably like Cyrus okay.'

'Cyrus wouldn't like my dad,' Harry says. 'Nobody likes my dad. He's a moron. I hate him!'

I split the rest of the evening between playing Xbox with Harry, and arguing online with Sandy Hammil. Then, somewhere around ten o'clock, this wave of massive tiredness comes over me, and I have to give up on the game I'm playing with Harry and throw myself down on the bed. The big orange shape looms large and all the noises in the house start to seem even louder, then I start to feel sick.

'Whereabouts in school is the library?' I ask Harry, just trying to keep a grip on things.

'Are you for real?' he says. 'You don't know where the library is?'

'I've just forgotten,' I say. 'It's a while since I've been there.'

He sighs in a kind of disgusted way.

'It's over in the new building,' he says. 'Upstairs from the computer lab.' But his voice sounds very far away. I think he keeps speaking and it all keeps getting further and further away, and the big orange shape gets bigger and bigger and I start to feel more and more sick. Then I'm asleep.

I have this dream during the night where I'm back at my own house and things keep getting broken, and falling apart. The walls inside crack and fall down, and the roof breaks too and falls inside. After a while, it's only me who's living there, and I wander about amongst all the broken stuff, not knowing what to do.

Then it suddenly changes to being this great big library room, where the books go all the way up to the roof, and everything seems very expensive and grand. I just stand in this place looking round at it all, amazed by the quiet. Even though I'm asleep I feel my body getting all loose and relaxed in the bed, and I start to feel great. I become convinced this library place is the place for me.

There's another bit later on that I don't really remember properly, but it doesn't last too long anyway. Soon Uncle Ray is up and about again, and before I know it I'm lying wide awake, staring at the ceiling, wondering where I am. And the whole mad experience of a day in the guardianship of my big fat crazy uncle starts all over again, somewhere not very far away from five o'clock in the morning.

25

By the time the morning break arrives, and I finally get a chance to go and check out the school library, I've been awake for so long I'm half expecting it to get dark again soon. I don't feel quite as tired as I did the day before though, and I can't wait to find out if the library has any of that quietness from my dream.

The frail-looking lady who's sitting at the front desk in there seems kind of pleased to see me when I go in.

'Can I help you find anything?' she asks, in a tiny whisper, and I wonder what the rules are. Do I have to let her help me find a book, or can I tell her I'm really only here to soak up the atmosphere?

'I've just come to work on my essay,' I say, and she looks quite happy with that.

'Let me know if you need anything later on,' she says, so quietly I can hardly hear her, and I tell her I will. She smiles and goes back to reading the massive book that's lying on her desk, and as I turn round for a look at the place I can't help but wonder what all the whispering's been about. Everyone else seems to be using the library for the same thing I've always used it for in the past: not being there. It's totally empty. There's no one but me and the library lady in here. So I find a desk up near the back, hidden in amongst some high shelves, and I take out my English jotter with all the Cyrus notes written in it, and just sit still for a while, listening.

I can hear a little bit of noise out in the playground, and now and again a door bangs somewhere far away in the corridor, but apart from that there's nothing at all. It's just like Mum said it would be. Totally quiet. My brain feels like it's wakening up, and all the little bytes start to chatter excitedly, as if they've been huddled together during a terrible storm and now they can come out again. I become convinced this is going to work out for me. I check my watch and see there's still a good chunk of break time left, and I consider asking the library lady for a book on pacifists, to see if I can find anything in there that will give me an idea for getting round Cyrus's parents, but then I decide to leave it for lunchtime when I can really get into it properly. This is really just a reconnaissance mission to find out if the rumours about library silence are true. I feel good about having had the idea, though, however small it is, and I write it down in the jotter, and then power through the rest of what's written in there.

Somebody else comes into the library after a few minutes, which annoys me a bit because I've already begun to think of the library as just being for me. I hear the door swinging, and then I hear the little snake-like noises of the library lady's whisper, although I can't hear anything she's saying from away down there.

'I'm fine,' a voice tells her, and the footsteps move up into the library. The little snake noises ring out again, and I suppose the library lady's asking the same questions she asked me when I came in.

'Okay,' the voice says, and the footsteps come even closer to where I am. I hope whoever it is won't choose a table next to mine. I don't want to hear them sniffing and shifting about, and turning through the pages of their book. But they keep coming. They come all the way up through the library to the shelves I'm sitting behind, and then I realise they've come to stand beside my chair.

It's this girl from the year above mine called Kirsty Wallace. She just stands there looking at me when I turn round, and I look back at her for a while.

'You the guy who's standing in for Chris Yates?' she asks. 'Over this fight thing?'

I shake my head. 'That's my cousin,' I say. 'I'm just planning it for him.'

'Well, we need to talk about it,' Kirsty says. 'We need to sort it out, here and now.'

'I'm busy,' I tell her. 'Find me at lunchtime. In the dining hall.'

She shakes her head. 'It has to be now,' she says. 'This is when we need to talk about it.'

Without me having heard a sound, a single footstep or even the sound of somebody breathing, I realise the library lady has suddenly appeared beside my table, and she's holding a finger up to her lips.

'There's no talking in the library,' she says, hardly even talking herself. 'I'm afraid it's not allowed.'

'Why?' Kirsty asks. 'There's no one else here.'

'You're both here,' the library lady explains, 'and the library is a place for studying. Not for talking.'

I start to realise that the library lady is my kind of person, and I have this vision of her coming into Uncle Ray's place and sorting out all the commotion for me there, until it's as quiet as the library. I wonder if she would do that.

'I'm sorry,' I tell her. 'We're finished talking now. I'll get back to my essay.'

'No you won't,' Kirsty says. 'And we're not finished talking. We haven't even started yet.'

'Then you'll have to do it elsewhere,' the library lady says.

'No we won't,' Kirsty tells her. 'It's a free country.' But I've already gathered all my stuff together, and got up from the table.

'Sorry,' I tell the library lady again. 'I'll come back later.'

'Thank you,' she says.

But Kirsty stays where she is for a while, asking the library lady if she wishes this was China, and if she wishes we lived under a totalitarian regime, then eventually she gives it a rest and comes out into the corridor behind me.

Kirsty Wallace is pretty strange. She always wears kind of, like, soldier clothes to school, and she has this rope hair she never washes. Sometimes her soldier clothes have camouflage patterns on them, and she's always having meetings for things she thinks are an injustice. The weirdest thing is, she's always trying to sort out things she thinks are unfair or horrible, but her way of sorting them out always involves doing unfair or horrible things.

'Why did you talk to the library woman like that?' I ask her out in the corridor. 'That wasn't cool.'

'What's it to you?' she says. 'Is she your new squeeze? Given up on Elsie Green?'

'I haven't got anything to do with Elsie Green.'

'Whatever. What you do in your private life isn't my concern. All I'm interested in is you standing in for Chris Yates.'

'I'm not. I told you that. It's my cousin Harry.'

'Either way,' Kirsty says. 'So where do you want to talk? Up in the common room?'

I look at my watch. 'I've got Science in a couple of minutes,' I say.

'Skip it,' Kirsty tells me.

Usually I wouldn't need any encouragement to skip Science. Any excuse would do. But talking to Kirsty Wallace, about whatever she wants to talk about, seems even less appealing than sitting listening to Baldy Baine making merry with the quantums.

'I can't do it,' I say. 'Baine saw me in the corridor before the break. He knows I'm in.'

'Your call,' Kirsty says. 'All I really need to tell you is you've got until lunchtime to do that stand-in thing in Bailey's office. You or your cousin Barry. Whoever. That's pretty much what it boils down to.'

'What's that got to do with you?' I ask her.

'We had a meeting,' she says. 'For the school trip. Everybody who's going on the trip, and everybody who's just tired of the crap. We're standing up. If you or your man don't step in now, we're all going to Bailey's office at the end of the lunch break. And we're telling him about Yatesy together. There's nothing him or his henchmen can do about that. Too many of us. People power.'

'But I'm still squaring the thing with Cyrus McCormack,' I tell her. 'I need to sort something out for Cyrus before he'll tell Bailey he fought Harry. If you go at lunchtime Yatesy gets expelled.'

Kirsty shrugs. 'He's standing in the way of the greater good,' she says. 'There are always casualties in the interests of the greater good.'

'Just give me a few more days,' I say. 'Then there don't need to be any casualties. What difference does a few more days make?'

'Can't do it,' Kirsty says. 'We're taking back the streets.'

'What streets?'

'It's a saying. It's a figure of speech.'

'It doesn't make any sense, though.'

'Of course it does,' Kirsty says. 'We're taking back the streets of Barcelona. For the school trip. It's over, man.'

I start to feel everything slipping away from me. Maybe she's right, maybe it is all over. The worst of it is, I know if I hadn't been farmed out to Uncle Ray's I would have a proper plan by now. I'd be all over the Cyrus situation like a rash. But even with my newfound quiet spot in the library, I don't know if I can come up with something even if she does give me a couple of days. Once my train of thought's been broken, all burst up by the noise and the chaos, it can take a couple of days just to get back on track, never mind to have the whole thing sorted out.

And then the bell rings.

'Enjoy Science,' Kirsty says, and heads off down the middle

staircase. I start running after her.

'Hang on,' I shout. 'Give me another couple of minutes.'

She slows down and I catch up with her before she's on the first landing.

'My cousin Harry doesn't get to university if this falls through,' I say. 'There are a lot of long stories involved, but think of all the consequences. Yatesy gets expelled, Harry's life is ruined. Cyrus too – he'll be high and dry. Think of all the good you'd be doing if you give me a bit more time. Who gets hurt if the school trip's on ice for a bit longer? It'll still happen. At least give me till tomorrow morning – twenty-four hours.'

I regret that as soon as I've said it. Twenty-four hours is as good as useless to me. I've got as much chance of sorting the whole thing out by lunchtime as I have of getting anything done by the same time tomorrow. But the thing about helping people out seems to have made a little dent in Kirsty.

'Let me see what my people think,' she says. 'Whatever they want, I'll go along with.'

'But you can convince them,' I tell her. 'Get me two more days. I'll tell Yatesy and Harry and Cyrus it was you who held back the mob, and you can take the credit for making Harry go to Bailey. You'll be feeling the love from all directions.' She thinks it through for a minute, twisting a big bit of her rope hair. Then she comes to a decision.

'Twenty-four hours,' she says. 'I like Yatesy – he's a freethinker. You've bought him a reprieve.'

'Give me two days,' I say, but it's not happening.

'Twenty-four hours,' she says again. 'Then we march on Bailey's headquarters. Tomorrow at thirteen hundred hours.'

It's a victory of a kind, I suppose, but it's as close to utterly useless as any victory could ever be. And I wander off to Baldy Baine's Science class in a state of total defeat.

26

I don't even bother visiting the dining hall before I head for the library at lunchtime. Trying to think on an empty stomach isn't always the best way to go, but time is so short I don't really have much choice, and I come out of Baine's Science class like a bullet out of a gun, breaking a world record for reaching the new block, and taking the stairs in there two and three at a time. I'd been hoping to get some thinking done in the Baldy One's class, but Sandy Hammil kept throwing dirty looks at me from the other side of the room, and Baine had us heating things up and mixing things together almost from the get-go, so I hardly got a minute to myself.

When I finally reach the library door I stop and look in through the little window, at all the silence waiting for me in there. I thought it might be busier at lunchtimes, but it's empty again, so I grab the door handle and get ready to feel the peace. The thing is though, the door doesn't open. At first I think I've just pulled it the wrong way, and I feel a bit stupid, but when I push it away from me the same thing happens. Nothing. I start pulling and pushing as hard as I can, till the door rattles in its frame, then I stop and bang on the window.

Someone walks up behind me and stops there.

'Keen today, Mr Dawson,' they say. 'I've never seen such a passion for learning before. Not in this school.'

I keep my hand on the door handle and turn round. It's my Geography teacher, Miss Voss.

'I can't get in,' I tell her. 'I think it's locked.'

'Of course it's locked,' she says. 'It's lunchtime.'

'So?'

'So the library closes over lunchtime.'

'But I need to get in. I'm working on an essay.'

'You shouldn't have left it till the last minute,' she tells me. 'Then you wouldn't need to work on it at lunchtime.'

'But it's not last minute,' I say. 'I'm making an early start on it.'

'Then you don't need to work over lunch,' Miss Voss says. 'Go and get something to eat.' And she wanders off and leaves me to stare through the little window at everything I'm missing inside. I can't work out how they get it so quiet in there. Out here in the corridor people are rushing about and chatting, their shoes clopping on the hard floor, doors banging everywhere.

'Can't you see I'm trying to think?' I want to shout. 'People's lives are at stake here.'

Out loud, though, I just shout after Miss Voss.

'Miss!' I call. 'What time does the library open again?'

She doesn't even turn round, just keeps walking. 'When lunchtime is over,' she says. 'One thirty.'

And I decide there's nothing I can do but head back to the dining room, and at least fill up my empty stomach.

I sit a few tables down from Sandy Hammil, and pretty

soon he starts giving me the evil eye again. He gives me it all through my war with the rubber chicken and the powdery chips, and by the time I'm moving on to the neon cheesecake I'm getting pretty sick of it, so I send him a text.

'I know you told Kirsty Wallace about Elsie Green and me,' it says.

'About your love affair?' he texts back. 'I didn't tell her. Or anybody.'

'She told me you did,' I reply. 'You're busted.'

'And you're a moron,' he says. 'And she's a liar.'

Then he gets up and leaves the dining hall, holding his middle finger up behind his back as he walks away. For a few minutes, I manage to convince myself I'll be able to think more clearly with him out of the picture, but my head is mashed. Digesting the road accident I've just eaten takes up most of my vital juices, and the noise in the dining hall starts to drive me almost insane. I've never really noticed it before, it was always just there in the background, but my experience at Uncle Ray's must have given me some kind of battlefield trauma, and I become aware of the full blaring cacophony – knives and forks on plates, the roar of talking and laughing and screeching, the cooks up at the counter banging dishes and trays and wheeling carts about, everyone's phones ringing and vibrating and beeping and playing music all the time. It gets so bad I even find myself thinking seriously about Uncle Ray's rope ladder scheme, and I try to modify it into some kind of workable solution. Maybe if I climbed up the ladder after Cyrus climbed out, and went into the bed instead of the pillows. Maybe that would be more convincing. And if I used a real ladder instead of a rope ladder . . .

In my crazy state of mind, this difference seems to matter somehow. I genuinely seem to believe the flaw in Uncle Ray's plan lies in the fact that it's a rope ladder. If only it was a proper ladder . . .

Just before I'm about to be taken away by a security patrol from a crazy hospital though, I see Cyrus coming into the dining hall and sitting down, and I dump my tray up at the counter then go and sit beside him.

'It's all over,' I tell him, as he tries to work out whether his chicken is real or not. He spears a piece of it with his knife and holds it up in front of me.

'What the hell is this?' he asks me. 'Is this food, or is it packaging the food came in?'

'I think that's the chicken,' I tell him, and he looks appalled. Then he pushes it into his mouth.

'What are you talking about, anyway?' he asks me. 'What do you mean by "it's all over"? It's been all over for me for weeks.'

'Not like this,' I tell him, and I explain the whole Kirsty Wallace thing to him. Strangely, he suddenly looks a lot happier than he did a minute ago.

'She's really going to do that?' he says. 'No bullshit? That sounds amazing.'

'No it doesn't,' I tell him. 'What sounds amazing about it? This isn't what we want at all, Cyrus. If Yatesy goes down, I don't help you get to the dance. Think of it that way.'

He shrugs. 'You'd never be able to pull that off anyway,' he says. 'No offence, but no one would. It can't be done.'

'Of course it can,' I tell him. 'I was almost there, Cyrus. This is the kind of thing I do all the time.'

He shakes his head. 'Not with my parents,' he says. 'No way.'

He struggles with another bit of the chicken for a while, then gives up on it and sees what he can make of the chips. I sit and watch him, numbly, searching through my broken brain for even the hint of an idea. Then I resort to begging.

'Please let Harry go to Bailey this afternoon,' I say. 'Then I've got all the time in the world to make sure you get to the dance. You can't let this thing get away from you, Cyrus. Think about Amy.'

He shakes his head. 'Kirsty's got a concrete plan,' he says. 'This way I'm guaranteed the bohemian's head on a spike. I can't pass that up.'

'But we're going to make sure we get Yatesy later. Remember? That was the deal.'

'I'm going with Kirsty,' he says flatly. 'She's got a plan, you haven't.'

'But I have,' I say. 'Listen, I'll give you an example of a rough sketch I've come up with for getting you to the dance. It's not ideal or anything, it's just to prove I can come up with the goods.'

He looks at me without saying anything, but I can't tell if that's because he's got nothing to say or if it's because the chips have formed into putty in his mouth, like they did in mine.

'Here's what you'd do,' I say, and in my desperation I lay out Uncle Ray's idiot plan about pretending to be ill. Substituting the rope ladder for a real ladder, of course.

He looks quite impressed for a minute, still trying to make inroads on the mouth putty, and then, when he's cleared a good enough space in it, he says to me, 'I live up on the tenth floor. Hillside Towers.'

I just stare at him. I find myself going down the bampot road of thinking about getting the fire brigade involved, or something like that. Surely Uncle Ray must know someone in the fire brigade.

'It's just an example,' I say, a bit too loudly. 'We're not actually going to use it. It's just to show you I'll come up with something.'

'It's the worst idea I've ever heard,' he says. 'I think you're losing it, Jackdaw. If that's the calibre of your thinking it's just as well Kirsty came along.'

'But I didn't come up with that,' I tell him. 'It was my uncle Ray. I've been living at my cousin's place, and my uncle's insane. And listen to all the forks in here, Cyrus. You probably haven't noticed it before but when you really start listening . . . And they close up the library at lunchtime. Did you know that? Two more days, Cyrus. Three more days. All you have to do is back up my cousin's story. Then my mum and dad will have sorted everything out, and I can go back home, and I'll come up with a zinger. I promise.'

He looks at me kind of sadly. 'You're freaking me out now,' he says. 'I've got to go, Jackdaw.'

'Everybody hates you, Cyrus,' I tell him, and he carries his tray off to another table and leaves me sitting there on my own. And I know that's the end of it now, no doubt about it.

I don't have the heart to skip Maths and spend the rest of the afternoon in the library. I know my wave of good fortune has run its course, and the way my luck is now I'd probably get caught and suspended if I tried it. So I do the zombie walk to the Maths class, and just sit in there watching pigeons out in the playground. I start to hope Cyrus doesn't tell anyone else about the ladder idea, I really don't want anyone to find out about that, and I try to think of a way to convince him to keep quiet about it. Then I find myself attempting to adapt it into something workable again, while Mrs Cunningham breaks out the quadratic equations or something like that.

I think Cyrus was right. I think I must be losing it.

When the bell rings for the end of the day I do the zombie walk again towards the school gates, and wish it was twenty-four hours later. By then Kirsty Wallace will have done her thing, Chris Yates will be expelled, Harry will be confined to a life of misery, and I can stop thinking of ways to get everyone out of it all. I can stop thinking about abseiling equipment and bungee cords, boom lifts and basket cranes, and numerous other kinds of mental ways to bring Cyrus down safely from a ten-storey window in Hillside Towers.

And then things get even worse.

I'm quite near the gates, just at the bottom of the slope leading up to them, when Sandy Hammil appears beside me and says,

'Heard you spent the day in the library. I heard you were studying love poems to recite for Elsie Green.'

I can tell he's just joking, trying to make me laugh so we can start being friends again, but I'm really not in the mood for it. He's got me just at the wrong point in time. And I smack him in the mouth.

He looks sort of stunned. He just stands there staring at me for a minute, as if he's not able to believe what's happened. Then *he* smacks *me* in the mouth. Hard. And then *I'm* kind of stunned, just standing there staring at *him*, even more unable to believe what's just happened. And then the crowd arrives.

Suddenly we're at the centre of an ever-expanding donut, and all I can hear is the sound of people running from all over the school, and the sound of those who've already arrived shouting, 'Fight! Fight! Fight!'

Nothing much happens for a bit after that. I stand looking at Sandy and he stands looking at me, and I hear people shouting things like, 'Hit him, Jackdaw!' and 'Kick him in the balls, Sandy!' But we both just keep standing there, looking at each other.

'I was only joking, you prick,' Sandy says. 'I was about to tell you I'm glad you're studying at last.'

'I'm not studying,' I tell him. 'Only pricks study. Pricks like you.'

'Use your own words,' he says. 'Don't use my words,' then he sort of comes at me. He starts pushing me against the wall of bodies behind me, and doing this weird dragging-me-about thing. I'm not exactly sure what he's trying to do, but I start pushing him back towards the wall of bodies behind him, and we struggle about like that for a good few minutes.

'Are you fighting or shagging?' somebody shouts, and somebody else tells me to put a thumb in Sandy's eye. But there's only really one thing I hear being shouted that has any effect on me. Something that starts with the randoms near the back of the crowd, and gradually makes its way forward. Just one word:

'Bailey!'

Then two words:

'Bailey's coming!'

I only become aware of it gradually, but as soon as I do I stop pushing Sandy about.

'Sober up,' I tell him. 'We've got to break it up. I'm on my final warning.'

'Good,' Sandy says, and he hits me properly then. Full in the face. I forget all about Bailey for the time being. All I can see is the red mist, and I hit him back. And I hit him properly now too. The crowd likes that, and the shouting gets wilder. Sandy grabs hold of me and starts doing the strange swinging-about thing again, and that's when I start to feel the crowd parting behind me. It's quite a bizarre sensation, but I know exactly what it means as soon as it starts. I know someone's coming through to the centre of the circle, and no one in the crowd has any intention of stopping them.

'We've got to quit,' I tell Sandy again, but he holds me even tighter, and swings me about even more. 'Get off me,' I say, trying as hard as I can to break free and do a Yatesy. But I'm too late. Before I know what's happening a man-hand reaches out and grabs me by the arm, pulling me hard and freeing me at last from Sandy's grip. Bailey's got me. He starts pulling me backwards so's I can't see where I'm going. My head tips back and all I can see is the sky, then he's bumping me through the crowd, smashing me off various randoms as we go, cracking me into their arms and their backs and their legs, while I'm struggling to get free, and still somehow believing there's a point in trying to make a run for it.

When we get out of the crowd I'm still facing the wrong way. I keep trying to turn round, but he's pulling me too quickly and it's all I can do to make sure a foot touches the ground now and again, while I continue to stare up at the sky. Eventually I feel myself being forced through a door, and pushed down onto a seat, and I drop my head forward and try to catch my breath. I feel badly winded. My face is alive with pain and blood drips down out of my nose.

I hold my nose shut with my hand, and then look up, look out of a window. I can't work out where I am at first, and then I have the most terrifying experience of my life. Everything outside the window suddenly starts rushing towards me, extremely fast, and I throw my free hand up in front of my face, expecting something to hit me. Expecting something to kill me. Nothing does though, nothing happens at all, and I slowly lower my hand again and realise I'm not in a classroom, like I thought I was. In fact, I'm not in any kind of room at all. I'm in a car. I'm in a car being driven down the road outside the school, at a breakneck speed, and it suddenly becomes clear that it wasn't Bailey who was dragging me about after all. It was my uncle Ray. The big fat crazy bastard. And it's his car I'm in too. His opera-star taxi. And he's sitting beside me crunching the gears and flooring the accelerator, and laughing like a hyena who's just heard the funniest joke in the world.

27

'Boy oh boy,' Uncle Ray shouts. 'You're the man, Jackie. You . . . Are . . . The . . . Man!'

I don't really feel like the man. I feel as if I'm about to burst into tears. My face is in agony, and my nose won't stop bleeding.

'What a punch!' Uncle Ray says. 'What a crack! You really showed that ball sack. You were on fire, Jack.'

'He's not really a ball sack,' I say. 'He's my best pal. Usually.'

Uncle Ray slaps his hands together. 'Fantastic!' he shouts. 'Even better. There's nothing like a good punch-up to deepen a friendship. You're a chip off the old block, Jackdaw.'

He takes one hand off the wheel and pushes my chin up without looking at me. 'Tip your head back,' he says. 'That's it. And pinch your nose. Now you've got it. Just stay like that till it stops bleeding. It won't take long.'

I hear him rummaging about in the glove compartment while I'm staring at the roof. There's a screech of brakes and the blast of a horn, then he drops a packet of hankies onto my lap and tells me to hold one up against my nose. He shouts out the window for a while, and when he's finished I ask him if he knows whether Bailey caught Sandy or not.

'I don't think so,' he says. 'I think he legged it. What's with that headmaster, anyway? What's his game? You've got to let a fight run its course in the playground. That's why there's so much disruption in the classrooms nowadays. Too much pent up aggression. If I was running a school . . .'

He carries on babbling while I fish out a hankie with one hand and take my phone out with the other. I manage to get the phone up in front of my face and send off a text to Sandy.

'Did Bailey get you?' it says.

If he did, it doesn't make much difference that Uncle Ray got me out of there before Bailey reached us. As long as he got Sandy I'm in exactly the same position as Chris Yates, and my long and illustrious academic career is probably at an end.

'Ten years I've been picking my boy up from school,' Uncle Ray continues. 'Ten years, and not once has he done me the honour of being in a punch-up when I arrive. But you, Jack! Two days! It broke my heart to have to pull you out of there. What were you fighting about anyway – a girl?'

'Probably,' I say. 'I don't really know.'

He sounds delighted. 'Fighting just for the joy of fighting!' he says. 'That's exactly the way it should be. Who needs a reason, Jack? Am I right?'

I want to tell him he's probably not, but it would be more trouble than it would be worth, so I just make a vague noise. He is right about one thing though, he certainly knows what he's talking about when it comes to fighting injuries. My nose stops bleeding in a matter of minutes, and I let my head fall forward slowly, keeping the tissue under my nose and waiting for it to start up again, but it doesn't. I pull down the sunshade with the mirror on it to have a look at my face, and it doesn't look as bad as I expected it to. It doesn't look nearly as bad as it feels, and it certainly doesn't look as bad as Uncle Ray's. There's no black eye, no swollen chin. Maybe all of that will come later, but at the moment it looks fine. I use the tissue to clean off the crusty blood round about my nostrils, then I push the sunshade back up again, while Uncle Ray carries on ranting about his pipsqueak son.

'Where *is* Harry anyway?' I ask, and Uncle Ray tells me he's walking home.

'He always walks when we've had a blow-out,' he says. 'He's a real huff merchant. Can't take a bit of fun.'

It's only then that I remember about the ruin of my grand scheme. All the fight madness had cleared it out of my head for a little while, but thinking about Harry, and the mess I've left him in, brings it all rushing back. And now I've got all that unhappiness as well as the pain in my face to contend with. Plus, I'm pretty sure Sandy's non-reply to my text means he's sitting in Bailey's office at this very moment, organising my expulsion. I stare out at the road and feel like bursting into tears again.

'I'll tell you what we'll do here,' Uncle Ray says. 'I'm going to take you to the pub, Jack. We'll have a few beers, have a few laughs. This calls for a celebration. You're a man now. No landlord in the country can refuse you entry to their pub this afternoon. I'll take you to Billy's place.'

Thankfully, he stops talking for a little while then. I don't know if I could have taken much more of it. Unfortunately, though, the silence itself is short-lived. Almost immediately he puts some opera on the car stereo, and starts warbling along with it, taking both hands off the wheel now and again to give full expression to whatever he thinks he's singing. I try desperately to come up with a way out of this pub thing, but we're already heading away from home, over in another part of town. He stops at a set of traffic lights, and I wonder if I could just open the door and run away. I could tell him later on I'd sustained a concussion in the fight, and went temporarily mad. Maybe he's so engrossed in the opera that he won't even notice I'm gone.

I look around at the street and wonder where I would head for, where would be the best place to take shelter. Then I see Cyrus out there. He's walking along the pavement with his dad, and he sees me sitting in the taxi and gives me the finger. I try to look at him in a friendly way, and give him a friendly wave, aware that I want him back on my side to prevent him telling anyone about the ladder idea. He keeps looking at me, as if he's trying to decide whether to return the friendly gesture or not, then he comes to his decision and gives me the finger again.

After that, all hell breaks loose. Uncle Ray starts blasting the horn and I totally jump out of my seat, wondering what's going on. At first I think it's got something to do with Cyrus giving me the finger, but it hasn't. He's blasting the horn at Cyrus's dad, and waving insanely at him, while Cyrus's dad gives a strained little smile and then tries to get on with his life. Uncle Ray's not having any of that, though. He rolls his window down and sticks the top half of his body outside. 'What's up, man?' he shouts. 'How are things?'

The lights change to green and cars behind us start peeping their horns. I haul Uncle Ray back inside, and he's got a big lunatic grin on his face.

'That's the guy I was telling you about,' he says, shouting over the opera that's still blasting out of the stereo. 'The mad bastard I told you about the other day.'

'The one with the tinfoil hat?' I ask.

Uncle Ray nods. 'Not that one,' he says. 'The other one. The one I told you about the other day.'

He eases away from the lights and rolls his window back up again. He's told me about so many mad passengers he's had in his taxi over the last couple of days I don't really know which one he's talking about.

'The one who collects old shoes, and turns them into plant pots?' I ask, and he shakes his head. 'The one that went fishing in the thunderstorm?'

'Not that one,' he says impatiently. 'The other one. The one I told you about the other day. Remember? The totally bampot one?'

And then he tells me which one he's talking about, and when he does . . . the whole world changes.

28

'Stop the car!' I shout. 'Stop the car, Uncle Ray!'

He looks at me as if I've gone mental, and asks me what I'm talking about.

'Just pull in,' I say. 'We're getting too far away. Stop here. Anywhere.'

There are some advantages to being The Man. Uncle Ray keeps looking at me kind of funny, but he slows the car down and pulls in. Then he turns to me as if he wants an explanation. He doesn't seem annoyed or anything, just curious, but I've already got my door open and I'm struggling to unfasten my seat belt.

'Come on,' I tell him. 'I'll explain the plan on the way.'

I hit the ground running and it's a good few seconds before I hear Uncle Ray's door slamming shut behind me. I have to slow down for a minute to let him catch up, then he's huffing and puffing beside me and I pick up the pace again.

'Remember my scheme?' I say. 'The one where I'm trying to get my friend to the school dance?'

Uncle Ray nods but he's already too out of breath to speak.

'That's him we just saw,' I explain. 'The crazy man from your taxi is his dad.'

I lay the whole plan out for him while we're running, and he seems over the moon. Once he's got it, I get back up to full speed and he starts to fall behind again.

'This is the life, Jackdaw,' he shouts, thumping along the pavement and breathing so hard I can still hear him up where I am. 'This is the life. What a day. *What* a day!'

But when I get back to where Cyrus and his dad were earlier, I can't see them anywhere. I look up and down the street, then I move from shop window to shop window, looking inside to see if they're there. They've totally vanished. I stand and watch Uncle Ray struggling up the pavement, his face turning purple and his hair all wet and sweaty. Then I look across the road, and there they are. I point towards them for Uncle Ray's benefit, and start weaving in and out of the traffic, being careful not to lose sight of them again.

'Cyrus!' I shout. 'Cyrus! Hang on a minute! Wait there!'

They're just approaching a parked car and Cyrus puts his hand on the door, getting ready to climb inside. I give him the extra-friendly wave again, in case he thinks this is anything to do with him giving me the finger, and I wish I could go back in time and not make up that thing about everybody hating him, in the dining hall. He stands looking at me and I do the friendly wave again. He still doesn't wave back but he doesn't give me the finger either, and I take that as a good sign. Then I catch up with him. His dad is standing on the same side of the car as he is, just straightening up after throwing something onto the back seat, and I hunch over and grip the top of my knees for a few seconds, trying to get my breath back.

'What is it?' Cyrus says in a nonplussed way. I get the feeling that he'd say something a bit stronger if his dad wasn't there. 'We're in a rush. What do you want, Jack?'

I pull myself into an upright position, and put one hand on Cyrus's shoulder to try and steady myself. His dad's looking at me curiously, and Cyrus tries to brush my hand away.

'Call me The Jackdaw,' I say, breathing heavily. 'Remember? Call me The Jackdaw.'

'What do you want?' he says again, having another go at removing my hand, but I'm holding on tight.

'I've cracked it,' I tell him. 'Everything's going to be all right. You're going to the dance, Cyrus. I can get you there after all.'

He frowns while he's looking at me, then he turns to look at his dad, as if he might know something about this.

'I'm afraid not,' his dad says. 'Cyrus has been grounded for two months. He won't be attending the dance.'

I give Cyrus a big smile and look across the road. Uncle Ray has just started crossing towards us, holding his hand up to stop the traffic as he comes. He looks like the craziest thing I've ever seen, with his big purple face and his black eye, the sweat dripping out of his hair and that big swollen gash on his chin. But he's grinning like he's never had so much fun in his life, and then he bursts into a few lines from one of his opera things, throwing his hands out in front of him like a maniac.

'That's my uncle Ray,' I say to Cyrus's dad. 'He wants to talk to you about Cyrus's situation.'

Cyrus's dad suddenly looks as if the roof has caved in, and I can tell he's realised his life has just taken a major turn for the worse. I pull Cyrus off to one side and leave Uncle Ray to do his thing.

'See my uncle Ray's black eye?' I say quietly to Cyrus, while the adults are conducting their reunion over by the car.

'Hard to miss,' Cyrus whispers. It's like Uncle Ray is a magnet for his eyes, and he can't look away from him.

I pause to savour the moment, then I hit him with it.

'Your dad did that,' I say. 'Your dad gave him that beauty.'

And the spell is broken. All at once, Cyrus only has eyes for me, and he seems pretty angry.

'No he didn't,' he says. 'My dad's a pacifist.'

I shake my head. 'Your mum's a pacifist,' I tell him. 'Your dad's a brawler. And that's why you're going to the dance.'

The anger becomes confusion, and Cyrus looks over at his dad and Uncle Ray again with this expression on his face like I think I must get in French sometimes, when Mrs Peterson is asking me a question. His dad and Uncle Ray are chatting away over there, Uncle Ray big and jolly, Cyrus's dad all punctured and defeated. Cyrus is finding it impossible to comprehend what's going on.

'Your dad was in my uncle Ray's taxi the other night,' I tell him. 'They got into an argument about Uncle Ray's opera singing, and your dad asked him outside for a fight. Your dad gave him that black eye and the big cut on his chin. Now my uncle Ray is telling your dad if he doesn't make sure you get to the dance, he'll come round and tell your mum all about the fight. How would she react to that?'

The light starts to dawn in Cyrus's eyes. He starts nodding, slowly at first and then it gets faster. 'She'd go through the roof,' he says. 'She'd never forgive him.'

'And we don't even need Uncle Ray now,' I say. 'You can tell your mum yourself if you need to. Uncle Ray just lends the whole thing a bit of authority.'

He grabs my hand and starts shaking it, then he does this strange little skipping thing. 'I'm going to the dance,' he says. 'I'm going. With Amy. I can't believe it. You're a legend, Jackdaw.'

I struggle to get my hand back.

'So we're on?' I ask him. 'You'll back up Harry's story? He can go to Bailey now?'

'Definitely,' Cyrus says. 'I'll even go with him. Whatever you want, I'll do it.'

I step a bit closer to him and lower my voice. 'Just don't tell anyone about that ladder idea from earlier,' I say. 'Keep that to yourself, Cyrus. I've got a reputation to maintain.'

'Understood,' he says, and I tell him not to say anything about the whole Bailey thing in front of Uncle Ray either.

'He's Harry's dad,' I explain. 'It's him we're scamming to get Harry into university.'

He tells me his lips are sealed, then he takes his phone out and makes a show of erasing the recording he made of me in the playground, the first time I spoke to him.

'No need for that any more,' he says, and I thank him. Then we stand together watching our dupes for a while. They're doing some kind of weird bear-hug thing, mostly at Uncle Ray's insistence by the look of it. Cyrus's dad squirms and writhes, trying to get free of the thing, and when it's finally over Uncle Ray gives him a big kiss on the cheek and slaps his bum.

'You're all set, son,' he shouts to Cyrus, and Cyrus gives me the thumbs up and runs off.

I watch Uncle Ray messing up Cyrus's hair, and generally abusing his Human Rights, while Cyrus looks half terrified and half elated. Then I decide it's time to finally bite the bullet and see if Sandy has replied to my text yet.

He has.

It takes me forever to work up the courage to open it. I stare at the little symbol for what seems like aeons, hardly even remembering to breathe. When I finally pop it open though, he's only sent me one word. It takes me a good few seconds to realise it's the only word that matters.

'No.'

I feel my whole body relaxing as the oxygen rushes back in, then I hear Uncle Ray speaking to me. I've no idea how he came to be standing beside me without me noticing.

'That's the most fun I've had in years,' he says. 'What a privilege to be part of one of your schemes, Jack. You're something else altogether. You're a one-off.'

He puts an arm round my shoulder and we watch as Cyrus and his dad drive away. Cyrus is giving us a big friendly wave, but his dad looks inconsolable.

'Poor guy,' I say, and give Cyrus the finger, just for fun.

'So how about that celebration?' Uncle Ray asks. 'Next stop Billy's public house?'

And the funny thing is, I don't even say no.

29

So all my dominoes fell, one by one, until Operation Naked Drew was back on again, after all. Cyrus kept his promise to back up Harry's claims, Harry took his story to Bailey, and Bailey bought it, wholesale, leaving Yatesy free and clear, and with no other option but to keep his promise to me.Not that he appeared to have any intention of trying to back out of it. The whole thing seemed to be right up his street. So we set it up for the weekend. Yatesy took care of arranging it with Drew, and I settled the details with Elsie, online, so's I wouldn't have to put up with any of her madness. Then it was just a case of waiting it out.

I spent the next few days just wandering around the school feeling the love. Cyrus couldn't get enough of me, Harry gave me the iPad back and told me I could do whatever I wanted with it, even Drew came up to me at one point and thanked me for the idea.

'What idea?' I asked him.

'The idea about doing a painting,' he said. 'For my girlfriend.'

I almost had a stroke at first, wondering how he could possibly know it was my idea, and thinking it had all gone wrong somehow. But it turned out he'd been getting apprehensive about going through with the shoot, so Yatesy had told him the idea was mine.

'No one's going to pass on a scheme when they know you're behind it, Jackdaw,' Yatesy said. 'When I told him it was one of yours all his doubts evaporated.'

Such is life.

'We're doing it on Saturday,' Drew told me. 'Wish me luck, Jackdaw.'

'You won't need it,' I said. 'Just make sure you look your best. Spruce yourself up like there's no tomorrow, and make sure your hair's on top form.'

I even managed to make things up with Sandy Hammil, over and above everything else. We met up reluctantly to go over our stories in case our names made their way to Bailey in connection with the fight, and before we knew it we were laughing away again. I think Uncle Ray was right. I think the fight has made us get on even better together. A bit like my mum and dad after some Special Occasion Madness. Without the kissing.

Speaking of which:

It's over! After one more night of insanity at Uncle Ray's the text message arrives while I'm sitting in Geography: 'You can come home now, Jack. Mum x.'

The Special Occasion Madness has run its course! That afternoon I come back straight after school, and I feel quite nervous when I'm unlocking the front door. The bonkers dream is still haunting me, I think, and I'm kind of expecting to find the place all desolate and empty inside, all broken up. Everything looks normal when I come in though. There's a crack in the bit of wood above the living room door that wasn't there before, but that's about it. All the walls are still standing, and the roof is still where the roof's supposed to be. Only my mum is in the house, though. She comes out of the living room while I'm hanging my coat up, and for a minute she just stands there looking at me. She seems kind of unhappy, and quite quiet.

'Have you lost any weight?' she asks me eventually. 'You look like you might've lost a little bit.'

'I don't really know,' I tell her, and she just looks at me some more for a while.

'Uncle Ray brought your suitcase back this afternoon,' she says. 'We'll have dinner in about an hour.'

There are a few things I want to tell her, and a few things I want to ask her about, but she's seeming kind of strange so I just go upstairs to unpack my suitcase instead. I smile a little bit when I get into my kid room though. Sometimes I thought I might never see it again, and I lie down on my kid bed and listen to the sound of Uncle Ray not banging any doors and not playing any televisions or radios as loud as they'll go. It's very quiet in there. And I enjoy not having Harry sitting at his chessboard all the time too.

When I unpack my suitcase I wonder for a little while what to do with the pouch full of golf balls. I consider going downstairs to ask Mum what she gave me them for in the first place, but then I decide against it, and when the suitcase is empty I just put them inside and zip it all up. Then I lie back down on the bed again, listening to the tiny kitchen noises and the no shouting or opera singing.

Dad still isn't there at dinner time. It's just Mum and me. There are no tiny cigarettes lying on the table, and there's no plate or even a mat to put one on round at Dad's chair. It's good to be eating something I can recognise though. Between the dinners at school, and the food at Uncle Ray's place, I'd forgotten that it is possible to actually know what you're eating, and for it to be a thing.

'Where's Dad?' I ask after a while, and Mum starts muttering about him, mostly to herself. For a bit it seems like she's not going to answer, then she pulls this note out of her pocket, and puts it down on the table next to my plate. It's folded in half, with just her name written on the part of the paper I can see, and she waves her hand across the top of it, letting me know that this will answer my question.

I don't really want to read it. The bonkers dream starts to haunt me again, and I try to just focus on my food for a while. Then I can't ignore the note any longer and I pick it up.

'Unbelievable,' Mum says, as I'm unfolding it and straightening it out.

'Blame Ray,' it says. 'It's his fault I'm not there. I don't know how to control him, Mary. He's dragging me out to celebrate Harry getting suspended from school today. For fighting. I'll try not to be too late, but you know what he's like when he gets started.' Then he's signed it, and Uncle Ray's signed it too, just to prove it really is all his fault. I start to feel a lot better. This huge wave of relief surges over me. I thought from the way Mum was behaving they might not have sorted it out this time, and that Dad might be gone. Now I see Mum's only annoyed about him missing out on the reunion dinner, and all at once the bonkers dream evaporates and stops haunting me.

'Did you know Harry had been in a fight at school?' Mum asks. 'Did you know he'd been suspended?'

'I knew a bit about it,' I say, and then leave it at that.

But you probably don't want to know too much about that stuff anyway. That's all just my own private beeswax. What you probably want to hear about is Operation Naked Drew. So I'll tell you about that now.

30

It all starts out beautifully.

I get to Yatesy's place about an hour before Drew is due to arrive, and we start working on our plan.

'I thought we could put Drew about here,' Yatesy says, and he drags a wooden chair into the middle of the room facing the window. 'That way there's plenty of natural light on him. It'll really help me to bring out the flesh tones. If I'm off to the side I won't cast any shadows, and then I should be able to get some really nice deep contrasts, just from the natural light and shade.'

It occurs to me that Yatesy isn't quite focused on the true purpose of the exercise, but I let it pass for the time being.

'Help me drag the easel over here,' he says, and we pull it close to the wall, then he tells me to go and sit in Drew's seat.

'Turn a bit more to the right,' he says. 'Put that leg further back.'

Then he comes over and shifts the seat about, and we have to drag the easel a few more centimetres away from the wall. Then he seems happy.

After that we get to work on setting up the hiding place for Elsie. Yatesy has these wooden things for hanging his clothes on to dry, like three ladders joined together. He's got two of them, and we arrange them into a shape so's they're like walls with a big space in the middle. Then we start hanging T-shirts and trousers and socks on the wooden bars, along with these big silk blankets he's got, so's you can't see through to the space in the middle. And when that's done we hang a big sheet over the top, like a roof, so's you can't see in from above either.

'How does that look?' he asks me. 'Natural enough?'

'Not quite,' I say, and I pull a few things about a bit, and rearrange the sheet so that it looks as if it really is just hanging there to dry. 'How about now?'

'I'm liking it,' Yatesy says, and he crawls inside by pulling two of the walls apart, and draws them back together again once he's in there. 'Can you see me?' he asks, and I study the thing from all different bits of the room.

'It seems fine,' I tell him. 'I can't see anything.'

'Sit in Drew's chair,' he says. 'Let me arrange it so's I can see you.'

I do like I'm told and watch some pairs of socks moving around on one of the ladder rungs. If I look closely I can see Yatesy's eyes peering out at me, along with half his nose and part of a cheek.

'How's that?' he asks.

'I can see you,' I say, and the socks start moving around again.

'How about now?' he asks. 'Any better?'

'That's fine,' I tell him. 'I can't see anything. Can you see me?'

'Perfectly,' he says, and he asks me to pass in the wooden box from beside the armchair. 'This'll be more comfortable to sit on,' he says. 'Pass me in one of those cushions too.' And when he's got it he asks me if I think we should put some food in there for Elsie, in case she gets hungry.

'She's not going to be in there *that* long,' I tell him. 'We only have to give her enough time to have a good look at Drew, then you can send him away for a break and get her out of there.'

He crawls out of the clothes-drier tent, and struggles to his feet. 'I'm just thinking ahead in case the painting starts to flow,' he says. 'If I get caught up in the moment it can carry me along for hours. Time doesn't exist any more. Not when I'm in the zone.'

Bohemians.

'We can't have her in there for hours,' I say. 'Drew can't sit still for hours either – he'll have to have a break.'

'Just to stretch, now and again,' Yatesy replies. 'Just a minute or two at a time.'

'Then you'll have to get Elsie out during one of those breaks,' I tell him, 'during the first one. Send Drew downstairs to the kitchen for something, or tell him to go to the toilet. Anything at all. The longer Elsie's in there the more likely it is to go wrong.'

He doesn't look happy with the idea, but he agrees to it. He keeps muttering something about his flow, and the dangers of making a shift to his left brain from the right for too long, but I keep on at him till he properly understands what it is we're doing here, and eventually I start to get through to him.

Half an hour in, and Elsie arrives, just as planned. She's really gone to town on her outfit for the occasion, even though she's going to be hidden away. She's wearing a green felt hat, with a red jewel clipped on the side of it, and her sleeves are enormous. She's got a purple waistcoat on, and a big pair of crazy boots, and something about the whole getup makes me wish I could draw a little black moustache on her top lip with a felt-tipped pen.

'Don't look into my eyes, Jack,' she tells me, 'you'll only hurt yourself.'

I don't even know if I had looked into her eyes, but I focus more firmly on her top lip and try even harder to imagine the little moustache fixed in place.

'Don't look at me at all,' she says. 'Allow yourself some mercy.'

Then she turns to Yatesy.

'Jack's passionately in love with me,' she says.

'So I've heard,' Yatesy replies, and I think he winks at me.

'Where did you hear that?' I ask him irritably. 'Sandy Hammil?'

'Everybody knows about it,' he says.

'You're gazing at me again, Jack,' Elsie says. 'Don't torture yourself.'

I try to put a halt to the craziness by showing her the tent we've set up for her. I show her the little seat in there, and she crawls in to have a shot of it. She seems to like it.

'Can you see all right?' Yatesy asks her, and she tells him she can see perfectly. 'Do you want me to put any water in there for you?' he asks. 'Something to keep you hydrated?'

She sticks her head outside and adjusts her hat. I realise I'm looking at her and quickly transfer my gaze to the carpet, just to make life easy on myself.

'I'll be fine,' she says. 'The sight of Drew will be all the nourishment I need.'

'Understood,' Yatesy says.

It can be very draining interfacing with the mad, so I do what I can to move things along and coax Elsie into position, then I close the tent up. After that my work is pretty much done, and I get ready to make my excuses and leave.

'Remember about the breaks,' I tell Yatesy. 'Forget about your left brain until Elsie's gone.'

He nods and I pick up my jacket. Unfortunately, just at that moment there's a knock at the door, and it turns out that Drew has arrived early.

I try to slip out just as he's coming in, but he seems delighted to find me there.

'I'm just leaving,' I tell him. 'Don't worry about me.'

But he's not having any of it. 'Stay for a bit longer, Jackdaw,' he says. 'I want to get your advice on this. I want to make sure we get it right.'

He seems quite nervous, so I agree to stay for a few more minutes. 'Just as long as I don't have to see you naked,' I joke, and he laughs a nervous little laugh.

'I've spruced myself up,' he says. 'Just like you told me to. Do I look all right?'

I give him the once-over and realise he's looking more polished than I've ever seen him before.

'You're looking sharp,' I tell him.

He goes over to look at a painting that's hanging on Yatesy's wall, not very far from where Elsie's tent is situated. I start to get pretty nervous myself, imagining I can hear Elsie breathing in there, and that I can hear the wooden box creaking whenever she moves. I'm terrified Drew is going to hear it too, and the whole thing will blow up in our faces. But Drew is completely oblivious, just staring at the painting on the wall, and then he turns back to me.

'Do you think I should look something like this?' he asks, and I nod.

'That's ideal,' I tell him and he wanders about looking at some more pictures in different parts of the room.

'Let's get you into the hot seat,' Yatesy says eventually. 'We'll run you through a few poses and see what Jackdaw thinks, then we'd better let him go. He's a busy man, Drew.'

Drew nods nervously and comes over towards the chair.

'Should we move this over to the window?' he asks me. 'Is this the best place for it?'

'This is the best spot,' I tell him. 'There's plenty of daylight here. That'll help Chris to bring out the flesh tones, and to get some natural contrasts.'

He gulps a bit at the mention of flesh tones, then he comes round in front of the chair and sits down. He crosses his legs one way then the other, shifting about uncomfortably, and then, suddenly, there's an almighty crash, like a bunch of fireworks going off. Drew almost has a heart attack, and jumps back up off the seat immediately. Even Yatesy looks startled. I scan the room at about a million frames per second, trying to work out what's going on. And what's going on, it seems, is that all the ladder things with the fake wet clothes on them have come crashing to the floor, and the box Elsie was sitting on has been kicked backwards and smacked down onto its side. On top of all that, Elsie is tearing across the room towards us, her face blazing with anger, while Drew experiences a second near heart attack, and flops back down onto the chair. Then he just sits there, with his eyes wide like saucers, staring up at Elsie who's screaming into his face.

'What have you *done*?' she cries. 'What crime of violence have you inflicted upon yourself?'

Drew looks as if he's about to start crying, and Elsie grabs the hair on both sides of his head, just beneath the ears, and demands to know where his tumbling locks have gone.

'You were an angel made flesh,' she shouts. 'Now you're nothing but a ridiculous schoolboy. This is awful. My love has flown.'

It's clear that Drew thinks he's just having a dream now, and that he's probably expecting to wake up at any minute. He seems to have gone into some kind of state of hyper shock too.

'Jackdaw told me to do it,' he manages to blurt out, amid his confusion. 'He said it would make the painting look better.'

Then Elsie turns on me, before I can even deny it.

'*You!*' she shouts at an ear-splitting volume. 'Your jealousy is without limits. You've ruined everything. Again. Never *ever* talk to me again, and you can forget all about me working on any stupid projects with you.'

And then she just screams for a while, very loudly, and when she's finished she runs out of the room in tears, and slams the door closed behind her.

The three of us stand and stare at each other for a few minutes, no one saying anything, Drew bewildered beyond belief, Yatesy looking strangely impressed. Then I tell them I'd better go after Elsie and try to calm her down, but I don't.

When I reach the front step I just close the door quietly behind me, and then I go home, leaving Yatesy to sort the whole thing out with Drew.

And the worst of it is, it all started out so beautifully.

31

So there I am, halfway through Monday morning, sitting on the steps outside the old building with Sandy Hammil, and telling him all about what happened at Yatesy's place at the weekend. Sandy's got a major crease on, choking on his bottle of water and generally making me wonder if someone who takes such delight in your misery can really be called a friend, when Yatesy's sister comes along and stops in front of us. She just stands there looking at me, waiting for Sandy to stop laughing and choking, then she says,

'Are you The Jackdaw?'

I'm not sure whether to say yes or no. I have the feeling that no good can come of me being who I really am. But before I can decide what to do Sandy says,

'That's him,' and I can feel another 'deepening of our friendship' coming on. I'm in for a surprise though.

'Thanks for convincing Drew to sit for that portrait,' she says. 'It's beautiful.'

It turns out that Yatesy just told Drew he'd had no idea Elsie was hiding in that tent thing.

'She must have sneaked in earlier,' he lied. 'She's been stalking you for months. She must have found out we were going to do this painting, and broke in somehow. Pretty scary.'

And Drew didn't bat an eyelid. He bought it wholesale, and then the two of them spent a pleasant afternoon getting on with the drawing.

'You've really helped bring Drew out of his shell,' Yatesy's sister tells me. 'He was always quite shy about his body before, but when he saw how much I appreciated the painting his confidence blossomed. We even went skinny-dipping last night.'

Sandy splutters a mouthful of water all over his shoes, and then looks up at me to see my reaction. But I'm becoming accustomed to the uninhibited ways of the bohemian, and I barely even crack a smile.

'He looks much better with short hair too,' Yatesy's sister says. 'He was starting to look a bit like a girl. Thanks, Jackdaw.'

'You're welcome,' I tell her, and then she's gone.

Sandy dries his shoes with the sleeve of his jacket, still chuckling away, then he takes a drink from his bottle of water and manages to keep it down for pretty much the first time all morning.

'I'll tell you what you are,' he says to me, and I look at him wearily.

'What am I?' I ask.

'You're a philanthropist,' he says. 'I've just worked it out.'

'What the hell's a philanthropist?' I ask. 'Is that the same thing as a pacifist?'

He looks at me as if I'm an idiot.

'Don't be a moron,' he says. 'A philanthropist goes about doing good for other people without wanting anything in return.'

I shake my head.

'I'm not that,' I tell him. 'I'm an ideas man.'

But he won't let it go. 'Look at the evidence,' he says. 'You've brought Cyrus and Amy together, you cured the rift between your cousin Harry and his dad, you've saved Yatesy from getting expelled, and you've turned Drew Thornton into a confirmed nudist. You've even managed to free Drew from Elsie Green's unwanted attentions, and what did you get out of it for yourself?'

He stops and waits as if he's expecting an answer, but I don't say anything.

'Nothing,' he tells me. 'You got nothing at all. There's no doubt about it, Jackdaw, you're a philanthropist.'

I ignore him and consider the position I'm in now, caught between the office and the factory, with the factory quite far ahead in the running, owing to my general lack of potential in the whole exam department.

'It's probably time to start hitting the books,' Sandy says, as if he's just read my thoughts, and I nod unhappily. I keep looking out over the playground and I watch a D-list seagull picking at an old piece of chewing gum that's stuck to the concrete slabbing. I wonder why the seagull's picked that particular piece of chewing gum over all the others, and then I wonder why it's trying to eat a piece of chewing gum anyway. Surely nothing good can come of that? The seagull seems to come to the same conclusion and hops across to a crisp packet instead, looking inside to see what's on offer. I watch its head jerking about, and look at this ragged bit on its wing, and then, without me even noticing at first, my fingers start to tingle.

It comes on slowly, first the finger tingling getting gradually stronger, then my head starting to buzz, and I suddenly catch on to what's happening. Incoming mail. I sit and wait patiently, giving it my full attention, and then it hits me with a bang. Almost as hard as the Elsie tent hit the floor in Yatesy's room. It's a mindblower. A real cosmic brain tingler. *This* is The Big One. *This* is the life-changer. This is the idea I've been waiting for all my life, and the app, it turns out, was only a warm-up. A dry run.

I look at Sandy and he looks at me, and after a second he begins to grasp what's happening. He starts to see what's going on. He knows I'm up and running again, and he shakes his head slowly.

'No,' he says. 'No, Jackdaw. Not again. It's time to get a grip on things. It's time to hit the books.'

I just smile at him, a huge smile. A great big Cheshire-cat-style grin. But I don't say anything else. I need to let this one germinate. I need to look at it from all angles and make sure it's really the game changer I think it is.

Then the bell rings. The bell rings for the end of break time and we get up and make our way across the playground, Sandy looking concerned, me almost skipping, and both of us off towards another mind-numbing double in Baldy Baine's Science class.

Acknowledgements

Thanks to my agent Joanna Swainson for finding a home for The Jackdaw at Hot Key, and thanks to Naomi Colthurst for all her hard work and enthusiasm for this book.

Thanks also to my Men in the Field: Marion Glover, Kirsty Brown and Kathryn Glover.

Stuart David

Stuart David is a Scottish musician, songwriter and novelist. He co-founded the band Belle & Sebastian (1996-2000) and then went on to front Looper (1998-present). He is the author of the adult novels *Nalda Said* and *The Peacock Manifesto,* published by I.M.P. Fiction in 1999 and 2001. His third novel, *A Peacock's Tale,* was published by Barcelona Review in 2011.

Stuart's memoir, *In The All-Night Cafe: A Memoir of Belle and Sebastian's Formative Year,* was published by Abacus / Little, Brown in 2015. *Jackdaw and The Randoms* is Stuart's first book for teenagers.

Don't miss The Jackdaw's second adventure!

Coming in 2016:

Jackdaw and The Ray of Light

HOT
KEY
BOOKS